THE HOUSE ON
BUZZARDS BAY

ALSO BY DWYER MURPHY

An Honest Living

The Stolen Coast

THE

HOUSE ON

BUZZARDS

BAY

DWYER MURPHY

VIKING

VIKING
An imprint of Penguin Random House LLC
1745 Broadway, New York, NY 10019
penguinrandomhouse.com

Designed by Cassandra Garruzzo Mueller

LIBRARY OF CONGRESS CATALOGING-IN-PUBLICATION DATA
Names: Murphy, Dwyer, author.
Title: The House on Buzzards Bay / Dwyer Murphy.
Description: New York: Viking, 2025.
Identifiers: LCCN 2024038409 (print) | LCCN 2024038410 (ebook) |
ISBN 9780593833179 (hardcover) | ISBN 9780593833186 (ebook)
Subjects: LCGFT: Thrillers (Fiction). | Novels.
Classification: LCC PS3613.U7284 H68 2025 (print) |
LCC PS3613.U7284 (ebook) | DDC 813/.6—dc23/eng/20240816
LC record available at https://lccn.loc.gov/2024038409
LC ebook record available at https://lccn.loc.gov/2024038410

Printed in the United States of America
1st Printing

The authorized representative in the EU for product safety and compliance
is Penguin Random House Ireland, Morrison Chambers, 32 Nassau Street,
Dublin D02 YH68, Ireland, https://eu-contact.penguin.ie.

For Carolina and Eloisa

THE HOUSE ON
BUZZARDS BAY

've been friendly with the same group of people for roughly twenty years. It began during college and continued in New York, and together we survived the usual city plights of unemployment, railroad apartments, income disparities, bad relationships, and good marriages. My wife was the last to join us. I was nearly thirty when we met. By that time the friendships had long since calcified, and it was fortunate she got along with the others so well as she did. We were married in city hall on a damp October morning and afterward held a reception at Callan's Tavern on East Sixth Street, in a back room built around a wood stove and what appeared to be a disused pulpit. Valentina's family was in Venezuela, and except for her sister they were unable to attend.

One by one my college friends, who were also my New York friends, the closest people in my life at that time and for some years after, climbed the wooden stairs very solemnly like a clan of Bay Colony ministers and gave their respective toasts, each finding something genuine and personal to say about my new wife. In the years that followed, Valentina forged her own bonds and shared memories and secrets with the others. When the twins were born, she was the one who suggested we make Rami the godfather. It seemed to me such an old-fashioned and touching gesture, and I worked hard to find a priest who would take us, two lapsed Catholics and their Muslim friend.

I don't mention any of this because I think it a great distinction to remain acquainted with the people assigned to your freshman-year housing. I only mean to impress that we were a unit and thought of ourselves that way and relied on one another to perform certain rituals and courtesies normally reserved for blood. When I was twenty-five and still in the throes of New York, I inherited a large house on the southeastern coast of Massachusetts, on Buzzards Bay. It had been built several generations prior by an ancestor with a penchant for gables and would have passed to my mother and father had they been alive. The town where it was built, Patuxet, was a small place. I knew it well, having spent summers there looked after by aunts while my parents were abroad. It seemed to me an eccentric and slightly disreputable thing, owning a beach house at such a young age, but it cost relatively little to maintain, and I couldn't imagine selling.

After six months of ownership and three blustery spring visits, when the bay was engorged and the locals all seemed to hurry about in sealskin, I came up with the plan that would later coalesce under the fairly ridiculous name of the Nanumett Sand and Swim Club, or the NSSC. I was just out of law school then and intoxicated with the idea of property and contractual obligations. I drew up the paperwork myself. The NSSC was a New York style co-op, except that the property held in common was a long stretch of Nanumett Beach, carved out from the plot I inherited, 137 Hazel Drive. I distributed four shares, one each to my friends, for a grand total of eighty dollars, and kept the fifth for myself. With the unanimous consent of all stakeholders, a sixth share was issued to Valentina after we were married.

Annual fees were seventy-five dollars, the collection of which was habitually waived, with proceeds strictly limited to beach upkeep and the purchase of towels and communal sundries. I suppose you could call it a ploy. At an age when it seemed less far-fetched to travel somewhere interesting in the summers, I wanted to improve my odds of having company on vacations and long weekends away.

As our twenties turned over and the demands of work and family drew us in new directions and away from New York, those beach summits kept us bound. It seemed a mercy, having people around who remembered how you'd been before the edges were smoothed. The house was large enough to fit the six of us and many more, but soon our schedules began to intersect less frequently. Rami went off to work for a series of trade commissions and moved for a time to Europe. His vacations were irregular. He would breeze in one evening unannounced and stay for an indeterminate number of days. Shannon and Maya tended to visit in August, but more and more we were a stopover on the way to Martha's Vineyard, where Maya's family rented a house.

Bruce was the first to abandon the effort altogether. He had never been very fond of the beach, though he accepted his share in the NSSC graciously and had the certificate framed in oak. Even on those evenings when the sun seemed to melt into the trees and our neighbors lingered on porches and brought chairs and drinks to the high ground over the beach to enjoy those obscure, evanescent moments, we would have to drag him out from whatever task he'd set upon in the house, usually a repair of some kind, though he wasn't especially handy and the constant disassembly and reconstruction of piping, garbage disposals, and light sockets never brought him anything but despair. He had been raised in Pennsylvania, in the hill country west of Gettysburg. The coast meant nothing to him. When he was young, he had gone to the Chesapeake for a week with his family, and he seemed to glean everything he needed to know of the Eastern Seaboard from those nights in his grandparents' bungalow eating boiled crab and stews.

As for Valentina and me, we took our summers seriously, more so after the twins were old enough to share the sentiment. The rest of the year we were a foursome of disparate tastes and inclinations, but in summer we all knelt before the same icons and said the old prayers to barefoot days and cool nights that sent you looking for a sweatshirt.

Valentina was on the law school faculty and tended to have July and August free. Occasionally her research assistants would come to stay, and we would do our best to show them a good and only slightly corrupting time. Rami might call ahead from Geneva or Istanbul, wherever he was stationed, and ask which students she had hired and what they looked like and whether they were interested in prematurely graying Arab men. Nothing much ever came of it. If it had, he would have told Valentina, and weeks or months down the line she would have mentioned it to me in passing as though surely I knew. They had an air of worldly conspiracy between them, always, and it gave the parochial New Englander in me no end in quiet, contrary satisfaction.

We tended to plan our first weekends in the house carefully and to dedicate the opening days to logistics, all the little chores required by life on the coast. There were errands to run, towels and sheets to inspect for moth damage, poison ivy to pull from between patches of grass, and then the house itself to look after: shingles to be nailed down, gutters that were inevitably clogged with leaves, and the water tanks, which were connected to a spring-fed well but managed to stink of eggs for two days after our arrival. I hadn't expected to relish those chores but over the years had come to. It wasn't the pride of ownership—I had no illusions there. The house was mine by chance.

That year we headed up the last weekend in June. The drive from New Haven kept to the coast. Once we passed New Bedford the land began to slope downward toward the lower sea basin. It felt as if the car could be shifted into neutral and we would reach our destination by fate. Normally Valentina would have dozed beside me, as the twins did in the back. Instead, we were discussing plans for the holiday and proposing little touches that ought to be added to the house to make things comfortable.

It was going to be the first time in several years that our friends, all the members of the NSSC, would come together under one roof. It was an unexpected moment. Until two nights before, we'd had no inkling that Rami would be back in the States so soon or that the house Maya's family normally rented on the Vineyard had been swiped out from under them. The chance that they would all three be coming for the same weeks in July was almost too abstract to consider, though not so long before, when we were all still living in the city, it would have been nearly unthinkable for an entire summer to pass without somebody getting hold of a car and hauling the others north for at least a week.

Bruce was going to join us too. He had called just that morning, surprising me. He hadn't been to the house in years. I waited until we were exiting the highway to mention it to Valentina. We talked it over and decided he would sleep in what we called the garden room. There was no garden but there were doors that opened to a yard, and he wouldn't have to look at the beach through his windows. There was an air conditioner, too, a window unit. It would cost me at least a morning to get it installed.

"How did he sound?" Valentina asked.

"Like himself. Like he was looking forward to seeing us."

It was a lie, but a small one.

"That's good," she said. "He must get lonely like anybody else."

The drive out to the house from the village center followed a dirt road that hugged the bank of a saltwater pond connected by inlet to the bay. The inlet spilled over like a great river delta into the marshes and attracted ospreys, which would circle overhead as you navigated the path's fissures. The salt in the air roused the twins, and we lowered our windows and let the din of the birds and the dust of the old road fill the interior. Soon a house appeared: our house, the silhouette of its roof peeking gamely over the pines. From the road it looked nondescript. Flourishes had been saved for what my family stubbornly called the front side, where there were gables, turrets, arches, and a roof that sloped sharply and curled back on itself like a Gothic cathedral. It was meant to make an impression on boats, and in fact we had a reputation as a useful landmark for lost sailors wandering toward the harbor's marina.

The sight of the house always quickened my pulse, but this year something was different. Valentina noticed it first: One of the screen doors was swinging open. The winter boards had been taken off in April and screens put in earlier that week by George, a reliably distant cousin whom we asked to look in on the place in the offseason. He was an old and worried man, and I couldn't believe he'd done anything so careless as leaving a door off its hook. I coasted into the driveway, which was made of seashells, and put the car in park but kept the engine running. The sound of the shells crunching under the tires ran a chill down my spine.

I asked Valentina to stay with the twins while I went inside. She hesitated, not because she believed I was overreacting but because she should be the one to go in. My eyes were never very sharp, and she had a near-perfect memory for people and spaces. In any case I went in and saw what had happened. The pantry was ransacked and trash strewn about. A hallway mirror was broken. A case of liquor we had stored the previous Labor Day was gone. There had been a break-in. Someone had been in our home.

I went outside, more startled than I cared to be, and explained the situation.

Valentina wasn't so concerned. She thought it must have been teenagers.

"You've broken into your share of cottages," she said. "You must have."

"Not recently."

"Come on, Jim. What else is there to do in these towns? The springs are so gray."

She was thinking of other towns: springs in Caracas, a riot of greens.

"They play bog hockey until April," I said, "then start swimming when the ice breaks."

She said if we didn't find condoms, she'd be shocked. We made a quick appraisal and decided not to call the police. There was hardly any real damage, only the mirror, a torn curtain, and the leg of a chair that looked as though it had been kicked out from under someone who had been seated there. For all I knew, it snapped under its own weight in winter. The wood got waterlogged and behaved strangely in the freeze.

"All in all, a pleasant trespass," Valentina said. "Fair enough. It happens."

The twins were still groggy from the ride and, after unpacking and checking on a few beach toys they had left behind the summer before, went to an early bed. They shared a room upstairs. In another year or two, we would make a new arrangement, but for now they could keep each other company and dream up stories for the sounds they heard in the night. The house made plenty of them. In winter it was worse, but in summer there was an unsteadiness to the structure, and big as it was, I sometimes found myself thinking of the old skeleton foundations you would see along the beaches in Falmouth, where hurricanes had come through and picked up houses whole and dropped them down ten, twenty yards away. Patuxet had been flooded but never felled.

I told Valentina I would stay up a while longer. She was tired from the ride and wanted to put herself to sleep making lists of what we had to do and buy the next day. Order had a reliable, sedative effect on her. Soon after, I found myself outside, empty-handed at first, then with a drink from a bottle that had been hidden under the sink. The drink made me listless, and I went inside for something else, something I couldn't decide on, then without thinking the matter through, I took a harpoon off the wall. It was an heirloom, passed down from a supposed captain several branches out on the family tree. How exactly it ended up in our house, or why I went to retrieve it that night, I couldn't say. It had been mounted somewhat haphazardly above a bookshelf in the living room. For as long as I could remember it had been there, and on many occasions I had thought about taking it down but had never done so until then. The barbs were dulled from time, but the weight alone could have knocked a man down. It was crazy to have the thing around the house. Crazy to display it. Crazy to go halfway around the world hunting whales the size of houses. The madness peeled back like an onion skin.

Around two in the morning I was still outside, rocking quietly on the eastern porch. Above me was the twins' room. I had the harpoon lying across my lap. I was thinking about whaling ships and the women left behind for years on end. Supposedly they paced those balcony walks and waited for husbands to return, but I didn't believe it. I was thinking, too, of the people who had been in my house and had walked my floors.

At a certain hour, you could almost see them, their eyes over the marshland, waiting. Waiting for what? For us to leave, it seemed: taunting us with their endless patience.

By morning things were less gloomy. There were no eyes in the tall grasses. I put the harpoon back on the wall and told myself I would soon store it in the far corner of the shed. The sun rose over the harbor, and it seemed a small miracle to have a porch that wrapped three sides of a house and showed the sun any place you cared to view it.

Valentina woke before the twins and came outside with a cup of coffee and the lists she'd made. Our day was planned out and the next one too: a full weekend, conceived in ink.

"Do you think we should get an alarm?" she asked. "For the house. Or maybe a dog?"

I told her we'd be fine and mentioned the harpoon. I had meant it to be funny, but she simply nodded and crossed the item off one of her lists. She was the only adult I knew who wrote in cursive. It was a florid, lovely script that always made me feel a little uneasy.

R ami was the next to arrive and had his choice of rooms. The house had three furnished stories, though hardly any of us ventured to the top floor, which trapped the heat and smelled faintly of an ill-advised wood stain treatment applied in the years before my tenure. He was fresh off a round of negotiations in Budapest and full of stories that flattered the listener by presuming at least passing acquaintance with the customs and quirks of Central Europe as seen through the refractive glass of international bureaucracy.

The first night we steamed lobsters. After dinner he helped the twins put on a play, a loose adaptation of Hamlet's *Mousetrap*, that petered out after the king's poisoning. He told us he had something important to discuss, but it could wait, and it did.

"Tonight is for the players," he said, meaning the twins, who were already jockeying for his favor. He always had a keen sense of the occasion and what was called for. It baffled me sometimes that he should carry on doggedly, year after year, showing up in our little backwater when he had the whole world at his disposal. He had been raised in

diplomatic circles. His career was the family trade. Maybe travel had
lost all its appeal.

We had all, in fact, studied to be diplomats, but Rami was the only
one who pursued it professionally. I found that rather odd, too, but
then there was the matter of his family and upbringing to recall, and I
was glad, anyway, that his and Valentina's careers occasionally inter-
sected and that they always seemed to have a great deal to discuss.

After the kids were asleep, Valentina asked him to give us the R-
rated version of Budapest, the commission, everything he had been up
to since we had seen him last.

"Budapest," he said, "is a convent. And not the sort you hope for."

Valentina was dubious, but he only shook his head and seemed to
be remembering something, another story he was holding in reserve,
perhaps, one he would let unfurl another night. Over his right eyebrow, I thought I saw a scar, though it was hard to be sure of anything
in the low light of the living room. We used very old bulbs that never
seemed to die. I couldn't remember the last time I had changed one.

Shannon and Maya arrived later in the week. Maya's family was
part of a prosperous community of African American burghers who
summered on the islands. I got the feeling both were glad to be relieved of the usual demands that went along with the summit. There
was also the matter of a strange incident, if you could call it that,
which had recently unfolded around them, and in which Maya for a
time had featured. She was an art teacher, primarily, with a growing
reputation for portraits. She would receive commissions now and
again and had begun exhibiting around the city. Earlier in the year, a
young man—an aspiring artist, apparently—began turning up at various shows and events she was expected to attend. He never spoke to
anyone but would place himself in conspicuous, unavoidable spots,

holding very still, in unnatural positions, for hours on end. Maya decided he was posing for a portrait, or in some fashion proposing himself as one of her subjects. She didn't like the young man. She thought
she recognized him but couldn't say for sure and didn't know where
from.

For three months, he kept turning up places where she would be,
going through the same routine. Then, suddenly, he was gone. A few
weeks later, word went around that he was suspected of having killed
his roommate. When they arrested him, the walls of the apartment—
in both bedrooms and in the shared living space—were plastered
floor to ceiling with Polaroids. The photographs were of Maya's work
and of the work of another artist she knew; a sculptor who sometimes
taught classes. The other artist, the sculptor, said he had never seen
the young man or the roommate at any of his shows and couldn't imagine how the Polaroids were made. Some portion of the work photo-
graphed was unfinished. Other pieces were finished but had never
been displayed. The young man died two weeks after the arrest: an
overdose, they were told.

The whole affair had disturbed Maya quite deeply, as could be expected. She hadn't been back to the city in over a month, though normally she drove down, for work or to see friends, at least once a week.
I supposed, given what I knew of the story and of Maya's possibly rec-
ognizing the man, it may have also contributed to her decision not to
go to the Vineyard that summer. Shannon liked it fine out there, but
for Maya it meant a stream of obligations and old acquaintances.
Also, she felt that her parents' friends were laughing at her for marrying a white woman. They would never come out and say it, not to her,
and not to her parents, but she was sure they were thinking among
themselves it was regrettable and amusing. It was a very cloistered

community, apparently. In any case, they had chosen to come to us when the family's usual house fell through. The plan, they said, was to stay for at least three weeks, possibly a month.

They unpacked in the same room where they had stayed the previous year, though then only for a night, on their way to catch a ferry in Woods Hole. I was glad they seemed to feel some possession over the space, or at least had pleasant enough memories of it to want to stay there again. The bathroom next door had two sinks and three mirrors placed at somewhat odd angles in relation to one another, so that sitting on the toilet you had a clear view of the back of your head, as well as a framed sketch of unknown provenance that hung on the wall above, depicting a child using a trainer potty while examining family portraits. The caption read, "Les affaires sont les affaires."

Shannon said it was the reason they wanted to stay there, near that bathroom: because of the art. I found a nightlight on the ledge and plugged it into the socket below the sketch. With the light cast upward, diffuse across the wall, it looked rather like a shrine.

Shannon said, "It's so lovely, James. Make one for me like that when I go."

Nobody called me James but her, and she only ever did it to tease me.

"You don't think Maya will mind?" I asked.

She looked at me uncomprehendingly. "Because of the portraits? In the sketch?"

"I just didn't know if they would remind her of . . . work. Or other things."

"No, James. I don't think she'll even notice. Not the way you're thinking."

I was glad to have them under our roof. Glad to be together again.

"Should we set her up a workspace?" I asked. "She could use the attic. Or I could see about clearing out one of the sheds if she'd like to walk to work. I always thought that would be nice, walking a few steps every morning, across a lawn, into your office."

Shannon said no, we shouldn't bother. "She's not going to work at all. If she does, I'm under strict orders to break her pencils. Burn her sketch pads. Take a knife to her canvases. Whatever's required. She's going to drink and stare at the sea and not think."

"She deserves at least that."

"She doesn't, but we'll give it to her anyway. What's a few weeks, unearned?"

Smiling, she kissed my cheek and wished me good night. She was quite tall. I didn't have to stoop for her to kiss me. She had been raised in Wisconsin, on a dairy farm. I met her family once and they were, all of them, six feet—the men and the women, the young and the old—or on their way past that mark. They were an exuberant bunch and always seemed to be organizing themselves to go elsewhere, to another house, where some cousin or aunt or uncle of great stature would soon be rustled up.

By Saturday, the house had taken on a new air of purpose, as though we were all engaged in some kind of agreeable business venture, like putting out a small newspaper. There were meals to prepare, dishes to clean, laundry to be done. The floors had gained a fine veneer of beach sand. Shannon was five months pregnant, and Maya was in the habit of worrying about her footing and of walking a step ahead whenever she ventured downstairs in anything but the full light of midday. They had been trying for quite a while, I gathered, and felt they may not have many more opportunities. I would sometimes notice Valentina watching them from across a room, Shannon in particular, and wonder whether she felt any envy toward them or only sympathy or some other emotion forever hidden from view. The twins were seven, and after a somewhat harrowing labor we had never discussed the possibility of having more. They were good, if slightly overmanaged, children. The plan that summer was to let them go as near to feral as possible.

It seemed a safe place to try. Patuxet was a remote, sea-dampened hamlet of nine thousand year-round residents, plus the summer crowds. On the village green was a memorial commemorating dead from the

Revolutionary and Civil Wars and across the street, by the stairs to the beach, a lengthier plaque listing fishermen lost at sea. The families who summered there tended to rent the same cottages and bungalows their parents had rented. There were a few inns along the bluffs to draw in weekend crowds. Main Street was painted every April, and by September the salt had done its work again.

We were waiting only on Bruce and, it seemed to me, anticipating his arrival with a certain high-strung excitement that bordered on trepidation. At school and in the years we spent living more or less as a group afterward, he could be a harsh judge of other people's pastimes and seemed always to be watching in your idlest moments. He had also, in intervening years, become somewhat famous. To my knowledge none of us had spent more than a few successive days with him since his first book was published. It was quickly made into a movie and afterward he undertook a series: widely read novels following the exploits of a philosophy professor who traveled the world and saved it from grave conspiracies, in between meals. The books made him rich, and a new one was released in hardcover every June. I had seen the latest just days before he called, as I was passing the windows of a bookstore not far from the campus gates in New Haven.

Rami and I went to pick him up at the town pier on an overcast Tuesday morning. The ferry sounded through the fog, and as it sidled up to the pilings the sun broke through and the passengers on the top deck were shielding their eyes as they looked at the widening sky and the town beneath it. The boat made the trip twice daily from Woods Hole to New Bedford and back, with a brief stop in Patuxet for no particular reason except it had always been that way. Only three passengers were disembarking. Bruce carried an overnight bag and seemed unsure of his footing on the gangplank. Rami waved and made a whistle to get his attention from the Jeep where we were waiting. We had parked just outside the pier on a small bluff where you could see the whole of the village center. We agreed that he looked good and younger than he had any right to.

"Remind me why he's on the ferry," Rami said.

"He went by fast boat to Woods Hole."

"From New York?"

"Long Island somewhere. Said he wanted the fresh air and time to think."

"Time to think. That doesn't sound too promising."

We got out and fumbled a little awkwardly over the hellos. I wished he had more luggage so that I might have taken something off his hands, but there was only the overnight bag, which he threw into the backseat and climbed in after. It seemed like something he had seen in a movie. Rami asked after the boat trip and Bruce merely shrugged and said it was smooth enough, but he hadn't expected it would take so long.

It was a six-hour trip, by my estimate, an hour longer than if he'd come by train. He was the last of us still living in Manhattan. He had a duplex with a key to Gramercy Park. Shannon and Maya had gone farther into Brooklyn, then eventually moved to Hudson.

During the drive back to the house, Bruce spread himself out across the back bench and dangled his legs over the sideboard. He was ready to relax, it seemed. The fog had burned off and the sun was singeing his nose. June had been hotter than the coast was used to. It hardly ever got above eighty, and when it did the breeze off the bay made it feel more tolerable, or pleasant even. I kept in low gears along the salt pond and did some lurching around potholes. I was used to driving an automatic the rest of the year, while the Jeep lived in a garage. The kids called it a beach wagon. We were rough on it, and it needed repairs every spring from a cousin who ran a body shop on Agawam Highway. I thought of it less like a car than as a boat, with all the upkeep that implied.

"I could give you some lessons," Bruce said from the backseat. "We'll do hill starts."

I told him to watch out for seagull droppings. We were all of us smiling.

"Guano is good luck," he said. "I thought you believed in the local lore."

"We had a break-in," I said. "They'd tell me that's good luck too."

"Maybe it is."

Rami had his seat reclined to ease the flow of conversation between us. We had the top down, and in fact there were seagulls circling overhead, riding the breeze up and down.

An osprey came over from the marsh, and its presence quickly cleared out the pack.

"Were they armed?" Bruce asked.

"They were gone. It happened before we got down. Teenagers, Valentina thinks."

"Bruce will solve it," Rami said. "He's a master of detection. I read it in *Le Monde*."

To this, Bruce said nothing. It was a proud, boastful kind of silence. I was glad for him.

There was, admittedly, a strange rivalry lingering between us whose exact origins and parameters eluded me whenever I got around to

thinking about them. Physically, we were somewhat alike and in college had spent a lot of time in the gym playing basketball and on the
track timing each other's miles to no particular purpose or conse-
quence. Bruce was more graceful than I was, but I suppose if put to it
you would say I tried harder. I think it bothered him that he didn't
have much dog in him. When we first met, I had a fairly thick accent
and he believed I must have grown up somewhere near the characters
in *Good Will Hunting*, a movie that was popular then. He seemed to
feel wounded, or deceived, when he learned that I wasn't from the city
at all, that I had grown up in different parts of New England, none of
them very tough or traumatized.

Our habit for a long time was one of quiet, determined competition with occasional score settlings. When we were first in the city,
after school, I wrote a short story that was somewhat improbably
published in a large magazine. It was a coming-of-age story about a
man and woman from the same town in Massachusetts living in New
York. For a long while I wasn't sure any of my friends had actually
read it, or whether I might have wanted them to. It seemed a slightly
affected thing to have done, and soon enough I went to law school.

Years later, nearly a decade in fact, when Bruce's first book came
out, I noticed his main character, the philosophy professor who was
originally from Massachusetts, had written in his youth what he referred to always and deprecatingly as a bildungsroman, which was
treated savagely by the few critics who bothered to review it. Somehow or another that failure set the professor on his course, and he
mentioned it often, as a kind of cautionary tale. It seemed to me a
pretty funny joke. I would have told Bruce I thought so, but he never
brought it up and for some reason I couldn't be the one to do it.

I meant it when I told him it was good to see him, that I was happy he'd come. He hadn't any brothers, either, and I felt we had always strived to fill that role for each other.

There was a genuinely warm welcome for him at the house. Afterward, he spent a great deal of time unpacking in the room we'd shown him to, the garden room. He had looked at it for a moment like he might ask to change. He could have stayed upstairs, but I doubted he would like it any better. In the end, he simply nodded skeptically a few times and said it was good of us to invite him. We hadn't invited him—it wouldn't have occurred to Valentina or to me—but the others were within earshot and perhaps he wanted them to hear. He seemed jumpy to me, though it might have only been the boat journey.

We spent the rest of the afternoon swimming and lying around the beach. I thought several times about going back up to the house to invite Bruce, but then I'd done that already and he had declined politely enough that I felt a little sorry about the intrusion.

----------◎----------

Before dinner we poured drinks and met on the lawn. Rami was the last to come in from the beach and said he didn't think he would shower; he would just let the salt do its work and see how things turned out. His hair was beginning to thin. In the dying sun, you could see the crystals of dried salt in the gray around his temples. It gave him a rather distinguished air, I thought. He seemed pleased with himself and almost drunk.

He wanted to know where the kids were so that they might finish their play, the play that supposedly he had worked very hard to produce and had to pull a lot of strings with the unions in order to open on time. He was doing his best impression of a New Yorker. For a diplomat, he was terrible at accents. They all came out sounding Russian.

"They're somewhere," I said. "A cousin's, probably. I don't know."

"You do know," he said, still in accent. "Jim, you must. Ve must all sink of ze children."

Sitting around the dinner table, which we had set up on the porch, I felt very glad about how things had turned out and also a little nervous that they should continue this way, and it seemed to me that the others—not only Valentina but also Rami, Shannon, and Maya—were feeling something of the same, and that we were all making an effort to put Bruce at his ease. It's often that way with staggered arrivals and group vacations. The ones who come before feel a certain obligation toward the stragglers. And then in our case there was the matter of Bruce's estrangement, which nobody at that table would have called as such, but it was the truth. He had pulled away from us over the years. Maybe he would have said it was all of us who had abandoned him. We had left the city, after all.

We were eating swordfish that I'd picked up that morning, which Valentina had grilled with olive oil and lemon. There was a simple salad beside it and on ice, in a cooler next to the table, several bottles of a Portuguese green wine that was ubiquitous in the local shops, whether or not they had a liquor license. It tasted a little sickening when warm but when served excessively cold had a distinctive, numbing flavor, almost like anise.

As the sun went down, I was feeling the effects of the green wine and the vanities of home and thinking that Patuxet might not be a very large or distinguished town, but it held its own against any of the most beautiful places I had visited. A little foolishly I was hoping someone else at the table might be feeling the same and would save me from having to say it. Mostly we were just catching up on old acquaintances and memories.

"I'd like to make a toast," Bruce said.

We had already finished three bottles and it was rather late for toasts, but he had pushed back from the table and was slumped down in his seat, a somewhat slack pose that boded well for our efforts to loosen him up. I was curious about what he had to say.

"To never changing," he said. "To keeping things just as they are and never swerving."

There was a baffling pause and a question in the air as to whether he was finished.

"May we live in museums of generations past," he said. "Next year in Jerusalem."

After another uncertain pause, Rami asked which Jerusalem he meant.

Bruce looked genuinely surprised at being questioned. His glass was near his lips.

"Mine," he said. "Yours. Our own private Jerusalems."

Following a long, rather bemused silence, during which we mulled over his meaning, Maya proposed we play a card game. Nobody was quite ready to leave the table just yet. The kids were home by then. They were upstairs, pretending to be asleep, discussing their own memories, their Jerusalems. Another bottle of wine materialized.

I went up to the pantry, where we kept the decks of cards and a coffee tin that was full of pennies. When I got back to the table, they had decided on playing blush, a nonsense game taught to me by my aunts, which I had passed down to our group. It involved licking the back of a card, affixing it to your forehead, then betting blind against the others for the high hand. You had to be well along in the evening to play a game like that. If you were and everyone approached it with a sense of lightness, it could be fun.

But we couldn't get the thing going. The cards wouldn't stick to Bruce's forehead. He kept trying, tilting them at different angles and holding his eyebrows still. He had a rather wide surface there, along the brow, which in other moments lent him an air of tremulous innocence. Now, it only seemed an obstacle: there was too much space to work with. Or maybe he wasn't using enough spit. Eventually, he gave up the effort and told us to go ahead, play without him, but by then the enthusiasm was gone. We decided it would be better to save the games for another evening, or for when it rained.

After the table was cleared, Rami drew me aside and asked if I'd like to go over to the beach. He was using his most discreet tone, and I thought I had better go. The beach was just a few steps from the house, across a narrow lane. There was hardly any moonlight.

"I think he's in a bit of trouble," Rami said. "Bruce, I mean."

"What kind of trouble?" I asked.

"Oh, I don't know. It's only an instinct. A suspicion, call it. Could be nothing."

"He was probably just dried out from the traveling and the wine."

"Not that. Something else. He seemed, I don't know, desperate somehow."

"Something with the new book?"

He shrugged. "I don't read the things. Do you?"

"Some of them."

"Are they any good? I've always wondered."

We walked a little farther along the beach toward a rock jetty. It was low tide and the rocks were exposed, but without any light they seemed to dissolve into the flats.

Apparently, there was something else Rami wished to discuss.

"I'm thinking it's time for kids," he said, pronouncing the words carefully.

He strained sometimes for notes of sincerity. His professional life bled into everything.

"I see you all preparing things," he said. "You and Valentina. Shannon and Maya. Sweeping the road clear ahead of you, accounting for everything. I'd like some of that."

"Will you get married first?" I asked.

Another shrug. "If I need to. I guess probably I do. Or they won't let me keep them."

"That's probably wise."

"But not necessarily. I think I would do well with a family."

"So do I."

"I wouldn't want to move them so often. Moving is hard on children. I'd have to pick somewhere to settle them. Some place decent but not too expensive. Geneva's impossible. Maybe somewhere in New England. It's worked out fine for you, hasn't it?"

We spent a while then talking through different parts of New England: Massachusetts. Maine. Not Connecticut, he said. He couldn't stand to be around anymore tax dodgers. In Switzerland, he said, everyone cheated on everything, most especially on their taxes. It had to do with the canton tradition and with the natural froideur of mountain people.

Later, as we were turning back to the house, he said, "I wonder how Bruce feels about it."

"About what?" I asked. I thought he might have meant the Swiss, with their proclivities.

"Kids," he said. "A family. I've never gotten around to asking him."

"Is he seeing anyone?"

"He hasn't mentioned it. There was some woman, the last time I was through New York, but she was young. It didn't strike me as serious. What do I know about it really?"

"I can't remember the last time he mentioned a girl."

After thinking it through for a time, he said Bruce was a wayward puritan. "A New Englander by inclination. And I guess he's always been a little in love with Valentina."

"Do you think so?" I asked.

"We all are. But don't worry, we'll never act on it."

"Oh no?"

He looked at me slyly, with a glimmer of appreciation. It was the setup he wanted.

"Ve must sink of ze children," he said. "Alvays ze children."

By the time we got back to the house, the others had already gone to bed.

4

n the mornings, Valentina and I had coffee and fruit in our room and took our time reading whatever had been left nearby the night before. I fixed the coffee in a press and carried it upstairs in a carafe. The assumption was that other people, our friends, would start the day in their own fashion, under their own steam, and we would meet later in the morning, on the beach or somewhere in the house, when it was time to rustle lunch.

The bed was large and comfortable and had a view to the bay. Its frame was custom built for the grandaunt from whom I had inherited the house. She had been in a long-term never-discussed relationship with a woman named Eileen, and I had come to believe the bed's inordinate size was their way of keeping room for the holy ghost, or its pretense, in the unlikely event that outsiders ever penetrated their inner sanctum. It took up quite nearly the entire room. We might have changed it for something more convenient and proportionate but never had. Valentina often kept papers scattered around its foot and picked up work first thing in the morning while I made the coffee.

It had always been that way between us: She lost herself in work while I navigated around. We met at a Christmas party in the federal courthouse in downtown Manhattan. I was clerking then with a district judge. She had been with the appellate court some years before. Somehow, I'd been roped into serving as bartender for the party, a rowdy, overserved crowd of judges, prosecutors, federal defenders, bailiffs, and favored clerks. She asked for a Negroni and came behind the card table barricade to show me how to make one. While the lesson was underway one of the prosecutors, a high-strung AUSA, snapped his fingers for my attention. She threw a bottle of seltzer water at his head and told him to fuck off. He did fuck off, and it was in the immediate aftermath of that encounter that I decided to love her. We were married within the year, and she gave birth to the twins exactly three months after the wedding. That was all in New York. I had never actually practiced law but enjoyed being around the courthouse clamor.

Later, we moved to New Haven and her reputation there was sufficiently strong from the beginning that she managed to find me some things to keep busy with. I taught a writing course for first-year students and ran an occasional seminar on literature and the law, the sort where we read *Bleak House* and the students spoke about their dreams.

I held on to no illusions that the campus elders would have afforded me even those modest roles except that Valentina had asked them to. She taught demanding, popular courses, was regularly published in the best journals, and was often brought in by mediation organizations to consult on border disputes. That summer she was, to her mind, between projects and had begun something new on a lark, an analytical piece on the legacy of a man named Herbert Wechsler, who was unknown to the general public but within the relatively cloistered world of legal scholars was a kind of titan. In the 1930s he had written a paper about the principles of homicide. After serving the prosecution at the Nuremberg Trials he came home and undertook to draw up a series of model laws. Apparently, his views about murder had changed during his time in Germany and that, I gathered, was the subject of Valentina's paper. She was an international law expert, and the Nuremberg Trials were the discipline's seminal event.

Coming back into the room, finding her still at work, always thrilled me. I never imagined having access to that kind of intimacy, I suppose. And then, also, there was something exotic and deliciously wasteful about lying around in a large bed, whatever the reasons.

She slept in nearly nothing, just a tank top and sometimes a pair of shorts, or not. That was the summer's effect on her. In New Haven it would have been flannels. At the beach it was too warm and humid for all that, and we didn't have an air conditioner in the bedroom and didn't want one. Her hair was tied up, her legs folded. I ran a finger up a bare thigh, testing the waters. It would depend, maybe, on the work. You don't expect the Nuremberg Trials to have any say in your sex life, but then you grow up, get married, children come: the world surprises you and it all seems a joke told in questionable taste.

"What are you laughing at?" she asked.

I hadn't laughed: Only my thoughts had gone in that direction, and she knew somehow.

"All right," she said. "Come on, then, show me what you had in mind."

She liked to be handled and tossed around, within reason. I was never perfectly comfortable with it but could summon the abandon in fits and starts. She had told me once about being choked, and what it felt like, done right. She had wanted me to, but the pressure wouldn't come when I had my hands around her neck. I couldn't squeeze hard enough. It was no good otherwise, she said, not unless I would pretend to mean it.

She lifted her hips for me to slide off her underwear. She had tan lines already: stark and slightly jagged. She said something I couldn't hear, and the thing gathered a sudden propulsion that surprised me. I had been expecting we would take our time but then she was pinned against that giant, ridiculous headboard and I was tearing at the tank top that was so flimsy. I wanted her out of that cotton. I wanted her to come pouring out of it. That was how I always felt with her: undone, overwhelmed, nothing.

Later, dressing, she asked where Rami and I had gone off to the night before.

"We walked over toward the bluffs," I said.

"But what was it he wanted to tell you?"

I described the plan he was hatching: kids, marriage, but nobody in mind just yet.

"He was probably probing," she said. "Checking to see if we have anyone for him."

"I don't think that was it. He did say he was in love with you. Bruce is too."

"Both at the same time? How do they expect me to get any work done?"

"A permanent condition, I think. Nothing to do for it. He didn't get into much detail."

She seemed to be thinking over the proposition carefully.

"Only if he keeps wearing the shorts," she said. "All through it. I'll need guarantees."

Rami had a pair of green shorts he had changed into the first night after arriving at the house, and which he had worn quite religiously ever since, taking them off only for a quick rinse and a spin in the dryer. They were his holiday shorts, it seemed: mint green.

"How would that work?" I asked.

"I don't know. That's up to him. He'd have to find a way if we're going to be happy."

She had put on jeans. She was going out for the morning. I didn't think to ask where.

Once, years before, we had all attended the wedding of a close friend. It was in a small town called Morzine, in the French Alps just shy of the Swiss border. Rami stayed in the spare room of a cottage Valentina and I were renting, about a half mile uphill from the village center. After the rehearsal dinner, the three of us were walking back to the house. The path ran along a ravine where torrents of snowmelt came rushing down the mountain. The embankment was steep and there were no lights to mark the way. You could hear the swell and the hurry of the cold water below, and the noise, which was thunderous at certain bends of the road, made it difficult to talk without shouting. We were walking three abreast along the path, with Rami on the in-side. There were no ropes or guardrails, just the path that was a mix of dirt and some gravel. At one point, a hundred yards from the house, Rami gasped and suddenly lurched backward. He lost his footing and ended up on the ground, about a body's length from the drop. It took him a minute to catch his breath and another minute after that before he could speak.

As we walked on, tentatively at first, he was laughing at himself, but he seemed to me quite shaken and unsteady on his feet. I thought it was only a bout of vertigo, which could have happened to anyone on that hill. He kept laughing and searching for the words to describe it.

Finally, he said he thought the two of us—Valentina and I—had planned something. The idea had overwhelmed him momentarily and frightened him.

"What do you mean, planned something?" I asked.

He was still grasping after it. "I don't know," he said. "To kill me there."

"To kill you? But why would we do that?"

Here, his laugh was more like a shudder. "I don't know . . . To get off, I guess."

To get off. What a mad idea. And how odd that he would feel the need to explain it.

Anyway, the memory of that night in Morzine came to me there in the bedroom, watching her get dressed in torn jeans, talking about Rami in his mint-green shorts.

There was no good reason why, but I thought maybe she was remembering it too.

5

Around ten I went downstairs and with the optimism of a coastal morning found Bruce and asked if he might like to go for a walk. He had mentioned wanting to see the town.

We shared a certain brand of restlessness, especially as the heat gathered strength. In college he had always been the first one up, and it was mostly the same in New York. He would cook eggs on a cast-iron pan and make coffee and lay out the table with books and encourage others to join him. I was the only one who did, usually. In those days he was reading books of correspondence between notable figures in history. He would read passages out loud occasionally, if he considered them especially worthy.

We went along Hazel Drive and took our time getting to the village center. By the pier, the beach was crowded and there was a trace of sunblock in the wind. We passed a cobbled square, and Bruce said somebody must have spent a small fortune sourcing the old stones. I told him it had been cobbled in the time when horses were still carting ice off the inland lakes and bringing them to the wharves to be shipped by boat to Boston and New York.

He just nodded and didn't seem to believe me.

We walked a little farther along the bluffs, and I asked if he'd like anything to eat.

"I don't care," he said. "What is there, anyway?"

At the lookout over the harbor there were two food trucks, a few scattered picnic tables, and, on the pavement just beyond the tables, a man on a bicycle that had been jerry-rigged to drag a cooler and a hot box. The man was standing on the bicycle's pedals, cranking them back and forth with a soft, uncanny movement that made the frame seem to tremble like a frightened animal. He was sunburned and scrawny. When he saw me, he waved. For many summers, I had been going to him once or twice a week for a sausage, but I didn't think he knew my name. All his regulars were called cuz.

"Cuz, I got chorizo and I got linguica and I got frankfurters but no buns, not today."

That was fine, I told him. I'd take a chorizo if he had a plate or a napkin to wrap it with.

"What does the big guy want?"

He was looking at Bruce, who was the same height as I was but always seemed a few inches taller. He held himself upright, like an officer going into a hopeless battle.

"Nothing, thanks," he said.

The man's name was Marcel. He rode his bike in a loop, dragging the cooler and hot box around the village. You could flag him down and he would stop and sell to you there, or you could catch him at the overlook or the playground or sometimes the pier.

I had been eager to bring Bruce here. I had thought he would appreciate it.

I ate my chorizo, the first I'd had that summer. It didn't taste the way I remembered from years past, and rather meanly I chalked up the difference to Bruce: his being there and not wanting any. Why couldn't he just content himself with whatever was at hand?

It wasn't fair to pin that on him, but I suspected already that it would be the first of many concessions considered and refused, and that if it continued, that same kind of thinking might spread to the group. Being together required a certain pliability if we were going to find any shape, let alone our old one, the one we had kept to for so long.

"How long do we have you?" I asked, trying to sound hopeful. "Days? Weeks?"

"Oh, I don't know," he said. He was looking down at the beach. There was a good crowd already and I felt like he was wondering about where they got the free time; whether they didn't have jobs to go to. He might have been thinking about anything.

I tried another tack. "Did you get much writing done this morning?"

He had mentioned that was what he intended: to write in the mornings, very early, while the rest of us were still sleeping. He hadn't said what hour that would be, exactly.

"No," he said. "I didn't."

"Did you manage to sleep in?"

"I couldn't get anything done. Not with all that noise going on."

He had paused over the word *noise*, considering how much disdain to pour into it.

He might have meant the children running around or Shannon and Maya clanging in the kitchen, drumming up breakfast. That wasn't what he meant, and we both knew it.

His room was beneath ours, and sounds carried through the old house.

"Oh," I said, and thought for a time about whether to apologize.

"I can never write somewhere new," he said, "not in the first days."

"Do you want a different room?"

"Let's see how it goes."

"Take any you like. You know where they are."

He nodded grimly, like it was an important allowance one of us had made, and got up to leave. I wasn't yet done with my lunch but decided it would be rude not to follow, and he might get lost on the route or pick a fight with a stranger over the cobblestones.

As we walked, he kept pointing to houses along the waterfront and speculating about what they cost in insurance premiums, one of the stranger topics of conversation I could ever remember settling on between us, but better than talking about noises overhead and what he had heard or not heard through the ceiling as he tried to write.

"You know you could sell your place," he said, "and make a killing on it."

"Why would we sell?"

He shrugged. The gesture had a strange insolence to it. "If you did, you'd make out well. You inherited it. You weren't expecting to. You got what you wanted out of it. You could do anything with the money. I don't know, buy an apartment in the city if you like. Hell, maybe you've already got money. I'm just saying, it's worth a lot, I bet."

We didn't want an apartment in the city. It seemed perfectly obvious to me, but on the other hand I didn't feel I could explain it to him. The truth is, I had thought about selling once or twice, but it had seemed rather indecent, grubby even, considering exactly what he had said: It was the house, and nothing else, that had been given to me.

The house was immutable. All houses feel that way to a degree. They should outlast us.

He wasn't in the mood to discuss abstractions, though. I could tell with him.

As we were approaching the house, finally, he asked me what I paid in insurance and taxes, and I told him the numbers. They weren't too extravagant, but he laughed and whistled, until I asked what he paid for his place on Gramercy Park, and he went silent.

"But that's different," he said.

"How?"

His face had suddenly turned serious. "That was a gift I gave to myself."

6

That afternoon, Valentina and I went for a swim. Once again, I truly didn't know where the children were. The sun had warmed the shallows, but out in deep water, it was cool as ever. Because of the sharp break and the draw of the inlet, it was always choppy near the shore, and there were strange currents that played across the body as you moved through. What it amounted to was a rather pleasant sensation of being drawn away from the land. If you gave a good kick at the right moment, you were propelled into open water. If you forgot the kick, the currents would grab hold and you would be swept fifty yards north, where the inlet gathered itself for the breach. Newcomers were sometimes wary of the water there, but we knew its movements by heart.

We went across the boating channel around the tip of Little Harbor. By car it would have been a long, dull journey to the other side of town. By water it was a straight shot of five hundred yards. The beach belonged to a seminary. In all my time swimming there I had never seen a monk or seminarian, but they had to be around somewhere, hiding in the woods, saying their prayers. There were more holy organizations nearby than you might expect. Patuxet had always been a sort of retreat. Wampanoags had used the land for rituals and fishing in summer. For a few decades there was a Spiritualist campground. Now there were two Catholic churches, one Pentecostal, one Unitarian, and one Episcopal, along with scattered outposts, like the seminary, which had likely inherited the land through an eccentric woman's final wishes, as I had mine.

Valentina stretched out on the sand. "You're not yourself around your friends," she said.

"They're our friends, aren't they?"

She nodded, a small point, but one she might have refused me in another mood.

"They helped form you. It's different. I met them when I was older. I'd seen things already, and there wasn't so much they could do to change me. It's simpler that way. Nobody's falling short of expectations. No need to look at the other and see your own disappointments reflected back at you. What you all have, it comes with more weight."

"I like having them around."

"Do you? I'm not sure. You keep so busy with them. You're always doing things."

"I'm hosting. It's been a long time. We're all trying to make up for it."

"What do you think will happen if you stop?"

I thought it over for a while but didn't have an answer. She had asked the question lightly and I tried to take it that way. I wondered if she knew where the twins had gone.

"I had an awkward conversation earlier," I said. "Bruce heard us, apparently."

"Heard us what?"

"This morning."

She turned over and undid the clasp of her top. "I've been in that room. You'd have to try to hear anything. It's removed. What did he do, climb the bed, put a cup to his ear?"

"I don't know. He alluded to it, pointedly. That's all."

"He imagined it. I'm sure he's wonderful at that sort of thing. A professional."

"He said he couldn't get any writing done. Not with 'the noise.' That's what he called it."

She smiled, shielding her eyes from the sun. "Is he trying to write while he's here?"

"That's what he says."

"Do you think he'll make us into characters?"

"Probably, if we keep it up."

The idea seemed to please her. She turned over and put the sun on her chest for a while. From the woods, I heard branches snapping and thought it might be one of the seminarians coming down to get a peek. It was only a deer, scared off at the sight of us.

On the way home, I fell behind. She was a naturally powerful swimmer. Through the academic year, she swam laps in the university pool and had built up a small coterie of undergraduate admirers. In summer, swimming in open water, she let go of her form somewhat and seemed to me faster and heedless. Most of the town was accessible by waterway, depending on tides. She would sometimes pick a point on one of the maps we kept pinned to a corkboard in the kitchen and, no matter the distance or weather, that was where she'd go, even into the open bay, farther than I would have dared. As we got older, I was awed by her recklessness. It was part of the power she held over me.

When we got in, the others were there on the beach. Except for Shannon, they were drinking gin and tonics. It made me glad to see them exercising their rights, the Nanumett Sand and Swim Club, the legal owners of all the ground beneath their feet.

They were talking about a class we had all taken at school, one that made a strong impression and had factored into our memories over the years. It was called Map of the Modern World. At the end of the semester, we were shown a series of blank maps and had to draw in borders and answer questions about disputed territories, mineral deposits, and historical successions. We had all studied for it together, every Tuesday and Thursday night, using flash cards. In those days, if you didn't pass the exam, they wouldn't let you graduate. It was something we had each had to endure, and I at least had always felt the cause would have been hopeless if we hadn't banded together for it.

We were better, it seemed to me, as a unit, and I sometimes wondered what I might have done with my life if we had kept together—if I had stayed in New York awhile longer, and they had too. It was an idle thought, one there was nothing to be done for.

From her beach chair, with a hand lying across her belly, which protruded very slightly, Shannon was going through the old drills, although without the flash cards. The names of countries she was rattling off were imaginary: Ravelstein, Penumbra, the Island Republic of Orinoco. It was precisely the tone we had always used to quiz one another, and Rami was answering almost as fast as she could ask the questions. I wondered how long they had been at it, and whether the gin and tonics were helping or hurting the effort. Bruce was sitting there, perfectly quiet. He had always been very competitive about our studies, especially when it came to that kind of core requirement.

"Mookie doesn't want to play," Maya said.

Mookie was a nickname she had given him at school. It was strictly between them. He had liked it, then. He thought it sounded like something an old ballplayer would go by.

"I'm waiting for it to make sense," Bruce said. "Then I'll play, I promise."

Rami said if he didn't know about the ports of Ravelstein, there was no helping him.

Bruce just shook his head. "I've forgotten more about Ravelstein than you'll ever know."

The ridges of his ears were burned, I noticed, and already peeling. He had fine skin. It always appeared that there was just that one top layer, and if you looked hard enough you could see right through. I found some sunscreen and offered it to him. He didn't want any. He said he never burned, not the way other people did, and we left it at that.

"In Ravelstein," Rami said, "the sun never shines, nobody burns. It's a gray nation."

For dinner, Maya took on the cooking and produced an eggplant dish that presumably was meant for Shannon and the baby's health, but which left the rest of us wanting. She was a terrible cook and ambitious in her failures—she would never have tried something simple. Yet her artwork had such restraint, and looking at one of her portraits made you feel as though you were seeing the depths of her subject's private life, and that what was really depicted on the canvas was precisely what did not appear.

Toward the end of the meal, the conversation gradually took on a more combative tone as we waited to find out whether there would be something more to eat or if one of us would have to sneak out later to buy a pizza. Bruce was asking Valentina about her work, at first exaggerating his ignorance and sounding like a somewhat naive first-year law student, one who hadn't yet mastered any of the finer points of constitutional or criminal law. But later, after he had drunk some more, the questions grew more direct.

He wanted to know about collective guilt and its legal foundation. This was in the context of the Nuremberg Trials. The philosophy professor who was the hero of his novels had completed graduate studies at a university in Germany. I always got the impression that Bruce believed himself to hold, at least honorarily, those same degrees.

Valentina was generous and patient with him. She laid out an engaging history of the law of conspiracy and explained why the Americans at Nuremberg had decided to bring the indictment on that count, which had to do with jockeying among the Allies.

Bruce had objections. To what, exactly, it was hard to say. He was fumbling after it.

"You have to admit," he said, "it's murky. To condemn one man for another's crimes."

Valentina smiled and managed somehow not to be patronizing.

"Sure," she said, "it's always murky. And we're always complicit. That's the beauty of the human condition, socially. We're a chain of instigations and provocations. Each of us is a link, always contributing to one another's downfall. It depends only on whether you're caught. And what kind of lawyer you manage to retain if you ever are."

"You can't really believe that," Bruce said.

It sounded suddenly urgent, as though he needed to know that she didn't.

Then her eyes narrowed, and she seemed almost to be looking past him, toward something in the middle distance that had caught her attention. Behind him was a dark stretch of marsh that was guarded over by a lone osprey perch. She asked why he wanted to know all this. Why the sudden interest in conspiracies and collective guilt?

He hesitated, then said, "It's for a book."

"Is it?" she asked. She sounded like she knew something, like she had caught him out.

He hardly seemed to believe it himself, and yet, why lie?

"Mookie's writing another book," Maya said. "Always another, and another, and—"

He turned on her sharply. "Could we cut it with this Mookie shit?"

She smiled. They'd always had an intensity between them that, from the outside, was difficult to interpret. Another form of competition, maybe, like the one he and I had undertaken over the decades. Once, he made a reference to them both being artists, and Maya outright laughed at the statement. He wanted to know what was funny and pushed for an answer, but she wouldn't give one. The laugh was a brief, involuntary reaction—it would have been cruel to put into words. Or maybe she was thinking of something else entirely, and I had misunderstood what was playing out between them.

"Sure," she said. "Go on, ask your questions, Mookie. You won't hear more from me."

"That's all right," he said. "I'm done. I heard what I needed to hear."

Maya reached for the water I had brought for the table.

"I wish I had that kind of cover," she said. "A novel. You can say any crazy thing that comes to mind if you're working on a novel and everyone assumes that's what it's about. It isn't like that with a painting. People think there isn't research at all. Just emotion. You don't get to ask anything, and if you do, you'll have to explain yourself."

Valentina offered a sympathetic look. "What would you like to ask me, darling?"

Maya turned to her with the same intensity with which she'd smiled before.

"Not a thing," she said.

"No?"

Maya shook her head. "I didn't go to law school for a reason. To hell with all of it."

I tried remembering whether she had considered law school. Most people we knew then had, but I didn't think she was one of them. One of us, that is. She had a plan, and it had nothing to do with diplomacy or maps of the modern world. So far as I knew, she never even sat for the LSATs. Anyway, what did it matter? We had all taken different paths from where we started. Life is meant to work that way. Time splinters us off.

———————○———————

I couldn't get to sleep that night and finally went downstairs and sat outside on the porch. The harpoon was there beside the rocking chair, leaning up against the rail. I could have sworn I'd mounted it back on the wall but evidently had forgotten to do so.

It was a stupid thing to have left lying around. I told myself in the morning I would mount it again, without fail, or maybe I would ask Bruce to handle it. It would give him something useful to do, although there was always the risk he would ask a lot of questions about whaling and my ancestors and then lie about why he wanted to know.

When my eyes had adjusted to the dark, I saw a figure at the edge of the yard.

I must have known immediately it was him because I wasn't startled at the sight.

Strange, that I had been thinking of him. I called over and asked what he was doing.

"Quiet," he said. "Come here, but keep quiet, for God's sake."

He was barefoot, as I was, and I could smell on him the green wine he had been helping himself to earlier, more than the rest of us, though I didn't think him drunk. I couldn't remember Bruce ever being drunk, in fact. He wouldn't allow himself that kind of license.

He pointed toward a dark line where the marshland met the pines.

"A coyote," he said. "He's waiting out there. I ran him off. He was on the porch."

"Just one?" I asked.

"On the porch, Jim. Not even afraid. He sauntered off when I charged out the door."

We had plenty of coyotes around. They came out of the woods. One summer, years before, there was a male who used to visit almost every evening around the same time, while we were cleaning the dishes after dinner. He had a spot in the yard where he liked to shit, and while he was at it, he would look through the kitchen window and hold my gaze. They were pretty meager creatures, there on the coast. Pitiable, in a way.

"I don't think he'll come back tonight," I said.

Bruce didn't seem so sure. "It could have been the kids who came outside, instead of me."

"They don't bother us. They're here for scraps, or a rabbit if they can get hold of one."

He just shook his head. It pained him that I didn't understand.

"You should build a fence," he said. "How can you have a yard without a fence?"

"Nobody has a fence around here. Anyway, there's the marsh and the beach."

"A lot of good they'll do."

In a way, I knew he was right. It was the same thing that had occurred to me that night sitting on the porch with my harpoon. I might have comforted him with a word of agreement but didn't. Instead, I left him there on the lawn, barefoot in the wet grass, still looking for some sign that the coyote was going to try to sneak back up on us, catch us unaware, a house of slumbering fools who didn't know what a fence was for.

7

When I was younger the Fourth of July never meant much to me. Once I had the house there was no getting around it. You either came at the thing with enthusiasm and energy or prepared to be swallowed. There was a relatively ancient if not formal right of way across the property that permitted anyone who cared to watch the town's fireworks show to gain access by passing through our yard and settling on Nanumett Beach. Over time, the rite evolved into an open house and finally a party, one that required or at least strongly suggested a great deal of food and a few hours of hospitality.

The prep used up a lot of hands. Even the kids pitched in and managed to move catering trays from the kitchen to folding tables in the yard without any major accidents. Ice was a thorny issue, always. I should have ordered it before but had forgotten, so Shannon and Maya went out and persuaded the manager of the bait shop at the end of Water Street that their need for it had something to do with the pregnancy. Chivalry or pity prevailed, and he had one of his guys fill up four coolers' worth and load it into the Jeep. There was gridlock in the town center, near the boat ramps, and the errand took them two hours, but they managed to see it through and came back into the driveway with the radio turned up loud, playing something wild and celebratory. Maya, at the wheel, laid on the horn and the kids ran outside to see what it was about.

The first arrivals came trickling in around lunchtime. It was hard to know who was there for the beach and who meant to stay the long haul into night. We put out sandwiches and salads to begin, and I got to work on other courses. Most people brought their own coolers to supplement whatever we were offering. There were contributions to the commonwealth too. Somebody brought a platter of stuffed quahogs. Duck Almeida, who had married one of the Thurgood girls, my second cousins, carried in a duffel bag from the Army Navy filled with Asian pears and lychees. He poured the contents into an old cranberry crate dug out from the shed, then went around showing people what to do with the lychees since they didn't seem to know. When there were no more takers in the experience of the raw product, he found a blender and got everyone rum drunk, using the lychee and pear juice to make mixers.

The barge puttered out into position around four in the afternoon. At nightfall, the fireworks would be launched from its deck, out over the water. One Fourth, years before, all the fireworks exploded at once, just when the show was beginning, and it caused a fire to break out. From the shore, you could see dark silhouettes against the flames, as the crew jumped overboard. Nobody was badly hurt, a minor miracle, and the next year they were back at it again. Ever since, there was an excitement in the lead-up to the show, especially once the barge was in position, and people would swap theories about what had caused the accident, what snuffed it out, finally, and whether it might ever recur. The barge itself was one of those old New England beasts proven more or less impervious to time, so long as only a few discrete tasks were asked of it.

It was hot all afternoon, and people were swimming. We put out towels because there were always a few who threw caution to the wind and came to the beach without them. An older woman I didn't recognize went around every hour or so and collected the spares and hung them to dry over whatever was close at hand: chair backs and tree branches, mostly. With all those colors flapping in the breeze, the place looked more festive, and I wished I had strung lights around the house as we had some years before.

Bruce wasn't much in the spirit of the day, I noticed. He helped me in the kitchen for a while, but the menu was so simple to accommodate the volume we had to put out, it seemed to lose his interest. I heard him say something curt about chicken thighs, and after looking over the sauces I meant to use, he showed himself out the back door.

We didn't see him again until dark. The beach, by then, had transformed. There were two hundred people or more packed into a stretch of sand which, even on a busy Sunday, rarely attracted more than a half dozen. Some had brought along spare furniture: not just their beach and camping chairs but patio sets as well. There were even a few old mattresses. It would all have to be dragged out that night. Whatever was left on the beach would be grabbed by the tide and drawn toward the marsh and deposited there or, depending on the currents that night, it might head off for Portugal.

It was turning into a gusty evening on the shore, while over the bay all appeared calm. The clouds hanging over the barge had parted, and the crew was starting the show, tentatively at first, maybe because of

past experience or because they had fewer volunteers these days. I had
seen a sign up in the village center asking for able bodies.

The buffet lines had long since cleared out. Even the lowly chicken
thighs in sauce had been met with what I deemed to be popular approval. I was feeling good and flush from the grill fires and the heat of
the kitchen and the warmth of the evening and went in search of the
twins so that we could watch the big fireworks together. They liked
the ones that fizzled like weeping willows, or at least they had other
summers. I couldn't track them down and settled instead for the last
of Duck Almeida's blender mix, which I poured into a plastic cup and
took on a tour of the yard, allowing myself to be trapped in conversa-
tions with distant cousins and neighbors whose faces I faintly recognized. People were discussing the wind, and some were questioning
the expense of the fireworks, though without much vigor, as the show
was going full tilt now and the explosions one after another had a way
of silencing doubts and inspiring a childlike wonder in even the mean-
est Yankee souls.

There was ash in the air, a light dusting that dissolved before
reaching the ground. If you held out your tongue, you could catch it
like snow and taste the sulfur.

On the beach, Rami was holding court. He had spent a good deal
of money buying fireworks for the house, a private arsenal stored under lock and key in an old gardener's shed the twins hadn't shown
much interest in since contracting two fairly garish poison ivy blooms
there the previous August. The crates had been hauled to the beach in
a rusted wheelbarrow. Now Rami was enlisting a few neighbors to
run extension cords from the house to two speakers he had set up in
the sand, just on the other side of the seagrass. He wanted to play music, in sync, while his fireworks were going off. I figured he had it

timed out so that he could go down the line with a good, strong lighter shielded from the wind, but he was short of cords by about twenty
yards.

It was shaping up to be one of those holidays where you lose all
sense of proportion, unless the thing can be brought back under control. If it can't, no one's the worse, really.

That was when Bruce pulled me aside.

"He's in no shape for this," he said. "Jesus, he can hardly see straight."

"What do you mean?"

"You know what I mean. He's out of his gourd. Tell him to quit it."

Earlier, behind the house, Rami and Valentina had smoked a joint.
I had noticed Bruce watching them from the kitchen, and the thought
of what judgments he might be making had annoyed me, though there
was no time to dwell on it, with all the cooking.

Valentina suffered from migraines and drank quite modestly as a
result. She enjoyed some weed now and again, especially during the
summer, when she was far from campus. She had those strong swimmer's lungs and could take down a reasonable joint in two or three
draws. There was showmanship in how she did it, and something ad-
olescent, too, and I was glad for her that she found her ways to relax.
Rami liked to join her in it whenever they were together. Probably he
was the one who had brought it.

Anyway, I didn't think it was Bruce's business what they smoked.

"He's fine," I said. "Look how organized he is. What could go
wrong?"

"He could lose a goddamn hand. He could burn the house down."

I didn't think so. Rami inspired in me a tremendous confidence.

"If he does," I said, "we'll find it. We've got flashlights in the shed.
Ice in the coolers."

"Flashlights? Ice? Are you serious? Goddammit, Jim. You need to think it through."

For some reason, listening to him made me angry: not that he would think me so callous, I didn't care about that, but that we understood each other so little these days.

"Tell him yourself," I said and walked off, leaving him there with his grisly ideas.

The fireworks came off fine, though without the soundtrack. Rami had kept his wits about him. He was a trained diplomat, after all. His moods and innuendos and indulgences were performed for the benefit of others. I loved him for making the effort, for the native generosity that sort of hammed-up acting implied. He wanted everyone to have a good time. He wanted music and fireworks to supplement what was already being offered by the town such a short distance away, and wasn't that a beautiful idea?

I had drunk a bit more during the show and must have been looking for Bruce to try explaining it to him that way, if he would listen. The party had started to break up. I found him standing near the water farther down the beach, away from the remaining revelers.

His pant legs were rolled, and the waves were washing over his ankles. His hands were in his pockets. He was looking out at the darkness that had so recently been flooded with color. More ashes were in the air and the wind was blowing them around like mad. It was blowing his hair around too. I noticed for the first time how it had thinned.

"One storm could come in," he said, "and take this beach out. It'd be gone in a blink."

"Or they could keep passing us by."

He shook his head. I had forgotten all about what I wanted to tell him.

"The winter storms are worse," I said. "We wouldn't know the damage for months."

"That doesn't bother you? Hell, it's your land."

"It's all of ours."

He snorted. A genuine honest-to-God snort. It pierced me straight through.

"Why did you come?" I asked. "Can you tell me that: Why did you come here?"

He didn't answer at first. It was something I had been wanting to ask but never found the meanness to put to him in so many words, although it had since occurred to me that he was waiting for me to do it, and every moment that passed by without me asking him was a sort of veiled insult. Sometimes that happens to a relationship. It doesn't matter what's spoken or unspoken, the insults pile one on top of the other. That's how marriages fall apart, I presumed. Friendships are just as precarious. That very idea occurred to me standing there in the mud. I could feel the pull of the water. The outgoing tide always felt to me stronger and more urgent, though I knew it wasn't.

"If you didn't want me around," he said, "you should have said so."

"It's not that."

"Then what? What do you want to hear?"

"I'm asking. I want to know. You don't seem to be taking much pleasure in all this."

"Is that what you think this is for? Pleasure? Jesus Christ, Jim, it's for pleasure?" He let go of a profound sigh. It sounded like he had more to offer on the subject. "Hell, I came to see you. All of you."

Just then Valentina came barreling through the darkness and across the shallows. The twins were in her wake. It was an exuberant, almost hysterical scene, as they kicked up water behind them and shouted at one another over the wind, which was gathering strength. They went out past the break, diving under the waves before they could swell.

It made me nervous to see them all disappear under the surface that way, into a deeper darkness, as though they might not come up again and I would be forced to endure it.

A night swim: Valentina always went for one on the Fourth of July. We hadn't discussed it, but I figured she had decided it was time to begin indoctrinating the twins into the practice. I was watching from that slight remove, no more than thirty yards, and thinking about stripping down then and there to join in: to join my family.

They hadn't seemed to notice us. I was about to go when Bruce stopped me in my tracks.

"You ought to watch after your goddamn wife," he said.

He had muttered it. There was something brutish and acidic and new in his tone.

I couldn't quite believe what I had heard and asked him to repeat it. I was daring him.

"Your wife," he said. "And those fucking kids. Swimming in the dark. Goddamn it."

It was like standing beside a stranger. A voice I'd never heard, never owed anything to.

Maybe that was why I didn't think much of taking a swing at him.

We had fought before, a few times that I could remember, at least twice on the basketball court, but this was different. It was a sucker punch, for one thing. Later, I knew, I would be ashamed for having thrown it, but in the moment it seemed to me almost a mercy, like it was what he wanted from me, and that he had spoken that way precisely in the hope that I would understand, and that knocking him across the jaw was the one good way to show him I did, the only way to get back on our old footing.

And in fact, I think he smiled as I connected. Afterward, certainly, he did, because I saw the glint of his teeth and of his gums as he lurched toward me. We went to the ground, to the water: into that murky in-between, a place that's neither land nor sea, where supposedly life began and organic matter is constantly being flushed through and transformed. My face was pushed down into it. I felt the water rushing up and almost washing over me but stopping just short, and then his weight was off me again and we rolled farther into the surf, where the waves were frothing and beneath us were stones.

"What the fuck are we doing?" he said, shouting. "What are we doing?"

He hadn't stopped, though, and neither had I. His knee found my side, and I reached over and groped in the darkness and grabbed something with my hand: it was a horseshoe crab's discarded shell, I thought, with that wicked pointer in front that looks so much like a knife. I held it over him and scared myself, knowing if it were made of harder stuff, if it had been a blade or driftwood or even a good hard clamshell I might have come down, and that would be an end to things: a brutal, irrecoverable moment.

I wanted to kill him. I had never wanted anything so much as that. It was rushing through my body and bursting out of the skin, like another digit or a limb I had grown.

Bruce had seen it too: had seen what I would do, what was in my heart.

We were tangled up still, practically one body. I let go of my grip and felt his slacken too. These things are over so quickly. They take years sometimes to begin, then finish in a flash: a moment so swift it's hardly even recorded. Blink, and you'll miss it altogether.

"I'm sorry," I said. "Jesus Christ, what is this? What am I doing?"

He was silent. It was a cruelty, that silence, and I asked him again.

His back was turned to me. I got the feeling he was counting off the seconds until some decent interval had passed and he could leave without conceding anything or acknowledging what had happened. He had such firm views on dignity and propriety.

That was what had started the whole mess to begin with, only I couldn't tell him that.

I couldn't tell him anything. We were strangers now. That much was clear to me, and I presumed it had occurred to him, too, as he left me there alone without uttering a word.

I sat a while longer in the mud, feeling ashamed and trying to calm my nerves. Valentina and the twins were still nearby, those thirty yards off, playing wildly in the water: splashing, diving under, and coming up again. They looked like birds out hunting for fish and paid us no more mind than birds would have if they found a spot they liked and were having luck with it. After a time, they swam back in and shared a towel. They were laughing at something, but I couldn't hear what it was over the wind.

I didn't go to them for fear that something in my presence would spoil things. I wanted them to have that moment with their mother: one good, pure memory. A summer night.

Instead, I cut through the seagrass and the salt spray roses and went around to the back of the house to clean off in the outdoor shower. A shower was what I needed. The water back there never seemed to get warmer than tepid, but at night, especially, it was such a useful thing to have around: a way of becoming human again. There was a fresh bar of soap on the ledge, the same type of soap we had been us-ing since I was a kid, and the faint smell of eucalyptus reminded me of my aunts, who would trudge out there for nightly ablutions all through the summer and fall, until the first frost drove them inside.

When I was done and clean, I went back to the lawn, where a small crowd was still lingering and chatting. Some of them were relatives who had their own memories of the house and felt, rightly, it was their prerogative to stay as long as they pleased on a holiday night, or at least until the booze ran out. There were some neighbors around, too, and the rest were strangers. I felt good and more like myself walking among them.

There was no reason to wonder or ask why they had come: They had always done so. I might have been one of them, and the fact that I owned the house changed nothing in their eyes or mine. That's what I was thinking, though the whole thing may have been nonsense, and I was still shaking free of that moment on the beach. I noticed some-body had built a fire on the sand. That was something Bruce used to do. Nobody asked him to, but he would spend an hour getting the kindling and tinder collected and arranged just as he wanted, and if the flames didn't catch straight away, you could see it caused him great pain, that he felt disappointed, not in himself or the firewood or the matches, but in the world at large: a world that had failed to meet its end of the bargain.

What could you do for someone who felt that way? Nothing, in the end. Leave them be.

8

The next day, Bruce didn't turn up in the kitchen or come outside to offer any help in cleaning the yard or the beach. I was relieved, in truth. I still hadn't thought through quite what I wanted to say to him and had a mean feeling he would meet me with a speech prepared and I would have to reckon with all my rough, half-developed notions in its wake. The day was fine and rather cool, and the beach wasn't in such terrible shape as I had imagined. At lunch we sat outside, beneath the elm, and ate cold chicken.

We were talking about the night before and all the people who had passed through.

Shannon mentioned that during the fireworks, she felt the baby kick. Now that she had felt it, unmistakably, she wasn't sure it had happened before, or if that was the first time. She had found the whole experience to be odd. Not at all what she was expecting.

"It was more like a knocking," she said. "Like somebody was at the door."

She held her belly as she spoke and I was thinking how she had always been such a healthful, beautiful woman, and I had failed to recognize it, and how there was something petty, almost squalid, in not appreciating a friend's beauty until she was holding it there before you, talking about it like that, in those hesitant, uncertain terms.

After lunch, she said she wanted to go for a swim. Maya was against it.

"Dr. Coogan said nothing new. No strange activities, things you're not used to doing."

Shannon smiled. "I've been in the ocean before, haven't I? What's so strange about it?"

"Come on, you're no swimmer."

They were gentle in their arguments. They always had been, in front of us.

Valentina offered to go with her and that put everyone at ease and off they went into high tide. They were holding hands as they carefully made their way over the band of rocks. That was where you began to feel the tide and currents grabbing, pulling at you.

After the first dive, they made quick progress toward open water. They seemed almost to have a particular destination in mind, as though they had been conspiring to go out alone, just the two of them, somewhere they could talk freely without being overheard.

Maya was feeling useless. I could tell, and she said as much after the girls had gone.

"I could disappear," she said. "It wouldn't matter."

I told her it always felt that way for stretches, then something would come up, something you were needed for. It would be obvious once the moment arrived. With Valentina, it was citrus. She couldn't get enough of it back when she was carrying the twins. It had to be fresh, so I bought a juicer and burned the skin from the backs of my hands with the acid from the runoff. I had been so happy, doing it. Perhaps those were the happiest moments of my life. It had all seemed so simple and brutal: twisting the rinds, being sure of collecting every drop, then chucking the spent carcasses into the garbage with a flick of the wrist, feeling good and dexterous and not wanting any of the fruit myself, but wanting only to see each one drained, bled dry. It wasn't just oranges she craved, but that was what I remembered. It was winter and we were in that small apartment. Coming in the door, it was all you could smell, like passing through a grove.

The lychees, the day before, had brought it all back to me. There were a few rinds still scattered around the yard. They looked like little snail shells that had been abandoned.

"Shannon doesn't like oranges," Maya said. "She never has. Not even those small ones."

"Clementines."

"Fucking hell, not even clementines."

"Then there'll be something else. Give it time."

"Sure. I know. It's just that . . . sometimes I want to snatch the thing."

"Snatch it?" I wasn't following her.

"Snatch it out, put it inside me. Then I'd decide what to douse it with. With orange juice, water, club soda, whatever I want. You can't explain that sort of thing to people."

She was drinking rum, a finger of it on a full glass of ice, sipping with an almost impossible restraint. She had gotten into the habit of fixing herself a drink that way every afternoon and carrying it around until dinner. While we were getting the table ready, she would chew on whatever was left of the ice. She must have been freshening it up over the course of hours, but I never saw her in the freezer, and it seemed instead she'd hit upon some kind of ingenious technique that defied physical law and kept things inside her glass perfectly intact no matter what melted off or was consumed.

I asked whether she was doing any thinking. "I'm told you're not to do any thinking these weeks. You're only supposed to drink and look at the water with an empty mind."

"Is that what Shannon said?"

"Dr. Coogan, I think it was."

"She thinks I'm taking things too hard, channeling all my angst into wanting to take care of my pregnant wife. She'd rather I paint something, but I'm not doing that either."

"Nothing new lately?"

"I used to work all the time, you remember? I always had a dozen things going. New studies or techniques to develop. That was the reason we left the city, in the end. I needed more space for all the stuff I was trying to keep up. But I don't want that anymore. I want to slow down and do exactly what I know how to do. It doesn't require all that preparation. All that failed stop-and-start bullshit. But she thinks it means something. She thinks I'm feeling dulled or stymied. It's the opposite."

She was looking down into her glass. Judging the ice melt, maybe.

"Then there was all that awful shit with the Polaroid taker."

That was what she called the man who killed his roommate. That mess in New York.

"Did you figure out where you knew him from?" I asked.

She shook her head. "I don't think I did, after all. He just reminded me of someone."

I waited to see whether there was any more she wanted to say on the subject.

Shannon would be upset if she came back from the swim and thought I'd been asking.

"He was creepy from the beginning," she said. "He had that young guy swagger to him, even though he carried himself like he was almost meek and wanted people to think of him that way. I got to know him a bit, from seeing him at shows. That was the point of him coming, I assume. Not to talk, just to show himself off, see what we thought. I thought he had that in him the whole time. If he didn't kill his roommate, it would have been somebody else. If it wasn't my paintings he was interested in, it would have been somebody else's. It wasn't about anything or anybody except him. That's what he wanted us to know. Or maybe I've been thinking too much."

"Young guys have that. All of them do. He was still, what, early twenties?"

"Twenty-six."

"They haven't lost it yet. It's not swagger, though."

"Then what is it?"

I didn't have the answer for her. I thought I did, but a moment later it was gone.

What was twenty-six like, really? I had known all about it once, or thought I had.

She was drawing lines in the sand with her big toe. Over her lap was a blanket, but beneath it she was wearing only a bathing suit. It was a warm day but slightly overcast.

"Maybe I'll start painting something," she said, "just to keep her from worrying."

"Do you want me to clear out some space for you?"

I described what I'd suggested to Shannon: an empty boat shed, a walk across the lawn.

She wasn't interested. "I'll feel obliged. That's the last thing I need."

I told her I wouldn't, but I was thinking maybe I would do it anyway, quietly.

"You could paint Shannon," I said. "Paint her five months in. Ask her to hold still."

She laughed, but I could tell she didn't like the idea. "No, I want to be paid. That's what it comes down to. If it sounds craven, why not, I don't give a shit. I'd rather pack my gear, take the ferry out to the Vineyard for the day, and do caricatures of my parents' friends. They'll all hang the goddamn things in their living rooms, next to the lighthouse paintings, and they won't know the difference except what they paid for it."

"It sounds like you've got a plan."

Her face turned serious. "No, I'm not doing anything, remember? No thinking at all."

On the horizon, you could just make out the girls by their bobbing heads. They were headed toward the same spit of beach where Valentina and I had been lying around. I told Maya about the seminarians who lived out there and whom I had always suspected of hiding behind the trees when swimmers came to shore to sun themselves.

"Have they got those funny haircuts, the monks?"

I told her I didn't know. I had never actually seen one. I only knew they were there. They were an article of faith. She laughed and said yes, that's exactly what they were.

9

We were all, perhaps, in a pensive mood and feeling languorous through the afternoon.

It wasn't until early evening, around six, when I finally went around back to dig up Bruce, thinking he would be at the desk we had set up for him, making a grand show of having worked the day away, just as he used to turn up at a meal with an ostentatious streak of grease or grime on the white shirts he wore while undertaking chores that never truly needed doing. I knocked at his door. There was no answer, so I let myself in.

The room had a stillness to it, as though it were preserved in amber. The bed was neatly made, and I had a memory of him telling me once that he had been prepared to enter one of the military academies, Annapolis, maybe, describing it as though there had been outside forces pushing him toward it, training him for something he couldn't quite fathom but which fate, in its wisdom, had chosen him for. In New York, he used to lay out his shoes beside his bed, like it might be necessary to jump into them in the middle of the night. He never seemed to think any of those little measures ridiculous, though he hadn't gone into the military after all or to any of the academies. Why, I didn't know.

In any case, I didn't see shoes anywhere or his overnight bag either. His charger was plugged into a wall socket, but there was no phone around. The desk appeared unused.

Gradually, it occurred to me he had taken off. The bastard had slinked away without giving me a chance to apologize, and without feeling the need to say anything himself.

It was so like him. In his absence, a judgment was cast: We had treated him rough. We had held him apart, and now he would do us one better.

No note, no goodbye. Just vanished in the night.

That bastard, I thought again, and wondered when he would come back.

Later, I explained it all to the others: what happened between us on the beach, what I found in his bedroom, or didn't find. In short, that he was gone, and I was sorry for it.

Rami said that he'd had one foot out the door from the moment he arrived. I shouldn't let it bother me. It wouldn't be a proper holiday unless a fight broke out now and again.

The others agreed. They didn't want me to carry the blame. He'd come around in a day or two, after he cooled off, got some sleep in a hotel bed, ordered himself a few dinners.

I had held back on some details concerning the fight: the brutality of it, however fleeting. There was no explaining it to the group. An urge like that is nothing, it's made of sand, there's no holding it, no way of gathering the grains once you've let them go.

Valentina must have suspected there was more to the story. In bed that night she asked me where I thought he had gone. Back to New

York? Or close by still? Maybe he had friends on the Cape that he had decided he liked better than us, or that he would pretend to like better for the sake of his hurt feelings. I agreed, it was possible. He hadn't mentioned anyone, but then he had hardly mentioned anything. For the life of me, in that moment, I couldn't remember anything we had discussed during his brief stay. It was like he had never been there at all. Except the others had been with him too.

"You take things to heart," she said. "He knows it. It was always going to be like this."

What did she mean by that? I wanted to ask but chose not to, maybe because I felt she was giving the matter merely half her attention, and yet she had it all figured out. There was always such assurance in her tone. In her lap just then was a book, the diary of a lawyer who had been at Nuremberg. It felt foolish, also, to be talking about my petty squabbles and worries beside such a thing, though she was the one who had put the book down in the first place and had prodded me lightly and asked for it: the real story.

And what had happened? Two old friends, having it out.

"Did you call him?" she asked.

"I tried."

"No answer?"

"I texted him too."

"So he's got you just where he wants, feeling guilty."

"It's not like I'm begging for forgiveness. I just want to know where he went. Why."

"But you know why. Why do this to yourself? You let it happen. You invite it."

"And you'd rather I had done what? Tell him off? Call him back for another fight?"

She said I was reaching now. Clawing at a new argument, one she didn't care to have.

I didn't feel like arguing either. In fact, quietly the awareness had been coming over me all through the course of the evening that I was quite relieved. Not only relieved, but genuinely grateful. With Bruce gone, already the group felt more like its old self, like something familiar and durable enough: It didn't ask for much, but only gave and gave.

10

That's how it was during the days that followed. We adjusted to the absence, forgot it altogether. Now and again, I would hear the crunch of seashells in the driveway and assume it was Bruce, but it never was, and I didn't send him any more messages or call.

New routines began to develop: claims on the day, its moments. They felt natural and timeworn, like paths through the seagrass. Mornings, Rami went out for coffee rather than having it at home. Shannon and Maya went straight for the beach to enjoy the early sun. Shannon wanted so much of it, Maya had to drag her inside for an hour of shade at lunch, and then they were back to it in the afternoon. Shannon's skin went pink, then settled, then her shoulders developed a sheen, like they had been polished.

She was swimming every day too. After, she would let the sun dry her off.

"If the baby doesn't want all that light," Valentina told me, "he'll let her know."

I noticed she had taken to referring to the baby as a boy. Had Shannon told her the sex?

"It's just how we would say it in Spanish," she said.

"Come on. You know something."

"How could I? They don't know themselves."

There was nothing to indicate she was lying, but I was sure of it. Little secrets, all around: Somehow, they never brought me anything but pleasure. It was the wonder of other people, how they dreamed things up in order to withhold them from you. Or maybe it was only marriage that went that way, if you were careful with it, and lucky.

There was so much Valentina hid from me back when the twins were coming. She had that old-fashioned instinct that told her there were bodily matters I shouldn't be privy to, or else she took me for squeamish. In comparison with her, I was. Her parents were doctors. Her father, a surgeon, brought her into operating rooms when she was young, on weekends in Caracas. She would scrub in and give him the tools. Her hands were always steady now. I couldn't remember a time when it wasn't true, when she had faltered or trembled. It was those Saturday afternoons in the operating room, which hadn't trained her so much as brought to bear an innate quality: a brutal kind of calm.

That was what she had brought to her own pregnancy, that calm, all through those long months. I used to find bloodstains on the sheets after they had been washed. Traces, spots, outlines. The stains still showed. I never asked about them and was ashamed of it afterward: how I wanted so badly not to know and had gifted myself that ignorance.

And now Shannon, too, seemed to me so assured. She hadn't been that way before.

"They should move here," Valentina said. "To the beach. Just stay in the house all year."

She meant Shannon and Maya. What an odd idea, I thought. Where had it come from?

"Shannon could keep swimming," she said. "Right up until the end. It's good for her."

"In winter?"

"When does the water get too cold?"

Weather, of all things, eluded her. In Caracas, there was no weather: just sun, warmth.

"But why would they want to stay here?" I asked. "They'd go stir-crazy. Cabin fever would settle in by October. By November they'd be running around slamming doors."

She wasn't buying it. She'd made up her mind, however implausibly, as to what was best. "It would do them good," she said. "We'd leave. It would be the two of them, then three. They'd have all these rooms to wander in and out of. And salt in the air. Babies get so congested at the beginning, especially in winter. The salt would help him."

"You're doing it again," I said. "Calling the baby a boy."

"Well, it doesn't matter. They'll go back to Hudson. There's no stopping them."

She sounded regretful, like it had already happened, we'd said our goodbyes.

She forgot what the coast was like in the offseason: how dreary the afternoons were and how, after the trees were rid of their leaves, the house was so exposed. We had made very few visits except in summer. Once, with a semester to myself and the kids starting in kindergarten, I had come alone for a stay of two or three weeks with the intention of beginning something new—a book, maybe—but had given up after four sleepless nights tossing around in that big bed, in sheets that never seemed to dry. The humidity was no different in the summer. It was worse, in fact, but you didn't mind so much when there was the promise of sunshine and other people on the other side of the night.

As for the four of us, the only time we had spent there in winter was after the twins were born. We went from the hospital to our apartment in Brooklyn and made a go of decorating for Christmas, but there was something inherently cheerless about the space, which was a railroad layout, one room opening onto another without any doors except to the bathroom. We owned a car by then and had the baby seats installed, so Valentina said why not spend the holiday at the beach? I didn't like the idea. There was no way we could bring all our equipment with us. She said, who needs equipment, people have been keeping babies alive and fed and happy without gyrating bassinets since the beginning of time. I could tell she had her mind made up, and that if I didn't go along, it would be the first disappointment of our new lives. For some reason I was resolved not to be the cause of that first disappointment. It seemed so important to me.

So we went to the house, bringing along rockers and a play mat. We set up in two adjoining bedrooms. The idea was that one of us would stay in the usual, enormous bed. The other would spend nights on a twin bed the next room over, beside the kids.

It was supposed to ensure that one of us, at least, would get some sleep.

What we didn't account for were the noises of the house, how the water gathering in beams and floorboards would seemingly be in a constant state of flux somewhere between freeze and thaw. The wood wailed under the endless gathering and release of pressure. There were drips, too, impossible to stop. You would hear them mostly at night, at odd hours. It was better sleeping in the room with the kids.

There, you could open an eye and be sure they were all right. But with a wall between, you never knew.

All through the night, whoever was alone would spend every hour jumping out of bed and running through the darkness to see what the matter was. A part of you knew it wasn't a sound a baby could make, it was something else, but that made it more awful.

And at dawn, we fought: vicious, half-sensible arguments. I still remember them as some of the most unsettling we ever undertook. We were always whispering, which made it harder, because when whispering you're always convinced the other person can't truly understand what you mean or want. One morning, after she had been alone in the big bed the night before, I went looking for her to begin the day's argument but couldn't find her anywhere and got annoyed and thought she was only delaying things. Once a routine takes hold, however unhealthy or unpleasant, you become protective of it and struggle for its preservation. It turned out she was on the roof. She had climbed out the window of the bedroom and onto a shingled patch beneath one of the gables. I used to go out there myself when I was young. It wasn't any great danger, even in winter, when there might be the risk of ice or something slick, but it made me furious, seeing her out there and I shut the window on her, trapping her. I had thought it would drive her mad in turn. She might break the window, even, and I wanted to see how she would do it: with a piece of clothing wrapped around her fist or with an elbow or a shoe. But she didn't move. She looked over slowly and saw what I had done and didn't care. She seemed almost glad that I had done it. She stayed out there nearly an hour, though of course I had opened the window again and she could have come in at any time.

After that, Brooklyn and the apartment without doors seemed it might be the better choice after all, at least until the kids were sleeping the night. The next winter, we were in New Haven, in a house, rented then bought: a small, sturdy, unlovely thing made of brick. There was never any more suggestion of spending Christmas—or even a long weekend—on the beach. We simply let the anticipation build and build, until summers arrived.

Why would she wish all that on Shannon and Maya, I wondered? She must have thought it would be different for them. Probably it would be. They had only the one baby coming, and Shannon really did seem to get some kind of comfort from the beach.

"There's still plenty of summer left," I said.

But she wasn't persuaded. "I want to do something for them."

"Like what?"

"I just wish they'd stay longer. Couldn't you talk to them?"

"And tell them there's a storm coming, ferry's out, roads are going to flood?"

"Think of something. It doesn't matter what. Tell them it's good for the baby."

11

That afternoon, I got it in my head that I was going to make a vat of orange juice. There was a juicer somewhere in the kitchen, I was sure. Worst case, I could use the blender and we would have a lot of pulp, or I would strain it out. I walked over to the market on Hawthorn. They had lousy produce but to get anything better you had to go to Stop & Shop, and for that you needed a car. Passing by the deli counter, Tom Shaw cornered me and asked whether I had heard about the kids they caught in the Canham house.

He was with three or four other men I didn't recognize and apparently that's what they were talking about. Tom had felt obliged for some obscure reason to include me in the conversation, maybe because he had been by the house on the Fourth and hadn't brought anything. He never brought anything but himself. He had a ruddy, worn face.

He said cops had arrested a group of kids squatting at the Canham house, out in Little Harbor, near the seminary. Six or seven kids, living together. He made some kind of gesture with his eyebrows to let you know what he really meant by that: *living together.*

Tom was an old Yankee, more in outlook than age. He said when they emptied the kids out before lockup, they had a pharmacy worth of stuff on them but not a single piece of ID. Nothing with a name on it. No birth dates, no credit cards, no insurance, no nothing.

"They were off the grid," one of the other men said. "Having a little fun, huh?"

Tom didn't seem to think there was anything fun about it. He had never felt that sort of pull, most likely. He was from one of those old families that preserves its inexperience of the world like an heirloom. He said it wasn't the first house the kids had tried either: Mrs. Canham hadn't arrived yet and might not come this summer at all, and somehow they'd figured that out, maybe just testing doors and watching out for lights until they found somewhere they liked, somewhere they could spread out and get up to whatever it was.

"Didn't you have a break-in?" Tom asked.

He was looking at me. The other men were too. They all vaguely resembled one another. They were men I had known, in one fashion or another, for years. Two of them I had known when we were kids. They were all wearing shirts with vented flaps across the back. It was the uniform among the locals. Their fathers had worn chinos and New Balance sneakers. In their eyes was a cold, hard look that wanted to pierce you through.

"George mentioned it," Tom said. "Mentioned you found a door off the hooks and some supplies raided, didn't know what to make of it. Well, there you go. Probably they were around your house first, digging up what they could. Shoot, they might have been making the rounds since spring. Kids like that, you don't know what they'll get up to."

He went on a bit longer, speculating about the things they got up

to. Apparently, when the police found them, they were all staying together in the living room. They had pushed all the beds they needed
into that one big space and were sleeping side by side.

The details were there, but the rest was speculation, and you could
hear that Tom was grasping after something more, something he
couldn't put to words or couldn't fathom.

He had a sister, I remembered, who went to California and never
came back. Probably she called or wrote, but they talked about her
obliquely, like she was in a sanatorium. Her name was Gretchen, I
believed. She'd moved to Rancho Cucamonga.

"No," I said, "we didn't have anything like that. No break-ins. No
squatters."

"What do you mean?" Tom asked. "George told me about it."

"He's confused," I said.

"Confused? You didn't have your doors off the hooks?"

"Hell, how many houses does George look in on? Wasn't ours."

I don't know why I told him that. Sometimes you just have an urge
to be contrary.

"Huh," Tom said. "Well, they've been around, believe me. This
wasn't their first stop."

He went back to speculating about what those kids were really up
to in the Canham house and whether they would make any of them,
or the boys anyway, do a little jail time to teach them a lesson. I said
goodbye and went off looking for the oranges. It turned out the market didn't have any. There had been a run on them, or maybe the holiday interfered with deliveries. Anyway, all they had that you could
make a juice with were apples. It wouldn't have had the same effect, so
I went home empty-handed.

———○———

When I got back, the girls were on the beach and Rami was off with
the kids looking for rock crabs. The way you did it was by digging up
fiddler crabs first, then tying yarn around them. Out on a jetty, you
could dangle the fiddlers down into the crevices and the rock crabs
would latch on. You had to be careful pulling them up, but Rami had
a light touch with it and the kids weren't bad either. With any luck, I
thought, they'd come home with a basketful. Nobody would be re-
gretting the orange juice then. Probably they hadn't wanted any to
begin with, but the idea had grabbed hold of me.

Shannon said they were waiting for me. They wanted me to settle
a debate.

"Tell us where he got those shorts," she said. "We need to know.
No more bullshit."

She meant Rami's shorts, the mint-green ones he had been wearing day after day, in and out of the water.

They seemed to think I would have the answer.

I told them I didn't know. Nobody could know a thing like that.
He might have had them made on Savile Row or found them in a Da-
mascus bazaar, it wouldn't have made a difference, because they were
his shorts, his holiday shorts, and they always had been.

"Jesus," Shannon said when I was done. "Do you really think he
had them made?"

She looked down the beach. He was coming back with the kids,
carrying a mesh net.

"I wish he'd had them made for all of us," she said. "That would
have been wonderful."

Valentina and Maya agreed, it would have been. They were having fun, laughing lightly.

I thought of telling them what I heard at the store, about the teenagers who had been arrested, but decided not to. It didn't seem the right time. Better to save a thing like that.

12

On Thursday afternoon there was a break in the routine. Maya wanted to watch the kids. They were old enough not to need to be bathed and dressed and lulled to sleep, but it sounded like that was what she had in mind in suggesting it. She would find out for herself, I figured, or they would lure her into a trap. They got up to things, those kids. Seven years old, but their craftiness caught you off guard, especially as it was two of them and they didn't need to exchange words to develop a plan of action or hold steady to it. In any case, Maya said what she wanted was practice: glorified babysitting. "I have to be ready soon," she said. "Better now, friendly terms."

The kids were in favor. They adored her. She was easy to love. She had a carelessness about her sometimes, worn lightly as a shawl, or like a skin she was in the process of shedding. "Go easy," I told them. They said they would. They were taking the idea seriously. A quiet look passed between them whose meaning I couldn't begin to grasp.

We decided on Vicino's Cafe, the four of us. It was a local place named after a family of Sicilians who had settled in the area generations before, first to harvest salt, then cranberries, then restaurants.

You could get a table and sit for hours, which is what we did, having too much to eat and a good amount to drink: pizzas, clam baskets, wine.

Shannon was eating tremendous portions, I noticed. I wasn't sure she was supposed to eat clams but figured they had been fried to hell and it couldn't really matter all that much. She seemed so content. She was the one who suggested ordering extras.

"I've never had bellies," she said, mentioning it several times, as though it were an unusual fact. Locally, people always preferred bellies to necks—the bellies were richer.

One of the Vicinos, the twin brothers who ran the place, brought another basket by himself and pulled up a chair from the next table over and sat down, straddling it, with his arms wrapped around the chair back. He was looking at Shannon's belly, smiling, and asked when she was due, whether they had a name, how they were planning to decorate the room. He said it was important to have the room decorated beforehand. You could tell yourself it wasn't, tell yourself this is just a baby, they're gonna be sleeping next to you the first three, four months in a bassinet, but having a room all set, decorated, was a meaningful thing, it mattered: "Everything matters at the beginning."

He was speaking so intimately, and Shannon was showing such concern for what he had to say, I wondered briefly whether they had met before. The man was about seventy years old. He had been running the restaurant for as long as I could remember, along with his brother. They were identical twins and would shout your name when your order was ready. They were always coming up with the most far-fetched pronunciation of whatever name you gave them at the register. It was a game to them.

I was never sure which brother I was speaking to, but I believed this one was Paul.

Shannon told him that in fact there was one thing they were hesitating over with the baby's room. They couldn't agree whether to install a camera or if they should use a simple audio monitor. Maya had the camera and had already connected it to her phone.

"But you," Paul said, knowingly, "you don't wanna do all that."

Shannon agreed, she was the one hesitating. She couldn't put her finger on why.

Paul said that it was sensible of her. Even a baby needs its independence. That struck me as a rather crazy notion, and yet I could acknowledge there was a certain sense in it.

He told her then about his youngest and how, when the kid first came around, they would leave him outside to nap, straight through the winter, so long as he was in the sun, and how it had given the boy a sense of himself, how he was in the world, and of his environment. "How's he gonna learn any of that if I'm watching him on a camera?"

He seemed to really want to persuade her, and she was taking it all quite seriously.

After he left, the conversation grew somewhat more subdued, until, after a long pause during which nobody picked at any of the clams he had left behind, Valentina took a particularly thick belly and held it up to the light. The batter was so fine, the light pierced it, and the clam, straight through. It looked more like a jewel, the way she was holding it. That must have been the fat, glistening. She asked Shannon if she had noticed Paul's hands. Shannon began laughing immediately and said of course she had.

"What about them?" I had to ask to be clued in.

"He kept reaching toward me," Shannon said. "As we were talking, his hand would leave the back of his chair and start closing the space between us. Like there was a magnet in them, or in me. You really didn't notice? It was so funny. I don't think he noticed either. But it kept happening. He'd draw back as soon as he got close to the belly."

Rami hadn't seen it either. It was like it had happened at a different table, to other people.

"I liked him," Shannon said. "I wouldn't have minded if he'd asked to feel my belly."

Valentina said he would come decorate her house if she liked. "He'll work all day, painting and hanging mobiles. Then at night he'll fry you the clams in a light batter. People will tell you it's a strange arrangement. You're not supposed to eat bivalves while you're pregnant, but that's just because they don't understand, not like we do."

Shannon was laughing. Valentina always knew what would make her laugh that way.

They went on for a time talking about Paul and what else he would do around the house, and Rami went up to the counter and ordered another basket, though we hadn't finished the one we already had. I think he just wanted to see how they would pronounce his name when the clams were ready. The girls were wondering about it too.

While they were waiting, Valentina announced she wanted to smoke a cigarette, and Shannon said she would go with her. She liked the smell. It reminded her of house parties and standing outside bars when she was young, something nostalgic like that.

I couldn't remember the last time Valentina had smoked a regular cigarette, but I figured she had her reasons, and I watched from the table, through the plate glass window, as she stopped the first stranger passing on the street, a young guy in swim trunks with no shirt, wearing a backpack, and got a smoke off him and a light. The kid lingered and seemed unsure whether he should stay or go, then eventually decided on the latter and walked into the road. There was a truck coming fast. I thought for a moment there might be an accident, something terrible, but the truck only made a hard stop and the kid got inside. It must have been somebody he knew, somebody who was there for him.

It was a strange evening, one that felt quite apart from all the others we'd had since arriving, maybe because it was the first time we had left the house and gone out to eat.

———○———

We went home along the beach rather than the road, approaching the house from its flamboyant side. We were walking in a line, for some reason, one behind the other, like soldiers marching, and now and again the leader would change without anyone discussing or deciding on it. A new body would slip the line and take over and veer us in a new direction for a time, down to the water or into the shelter at the base of the bluffs. We weren't talking much anymore. We had talked a great deal over dinner.

When we got inside, things took a turn. There was a woman there with Maya. A rather refined woman in immaculate white pants and a blue silk shirt, sitting in the living room on the plaid couch that I had always hated but never got around to replacing. She was holding a glass of wine. Her shoes were kicked off. If Maya hadn't been there, I might have thought we'd gone into the wrong house. I had done that once, when I was younger, after I first took over the place. Coming home by the beach in a rather dense fog with plenty of liquor in me, I had climbed the bluffs too soon and mindlessly let myself in the wrong door. I lay down on a couch and tried for maybe a half hour to sleep, but it wouldn't come, and when I got up to use a bathroom, I saw pictures on the wall, realized the mistake, and managed to go before anyone called the police.

But now, I wasn't in the wrong house. This was a stranger, sitting in mine.

After what seemed to me a very long delay, the woman turned and cast an indulgent smile in our direction. She didn't stand or put down her glass or betray any kind of awkwardness. She only held out her arms, as if she meant to grab each of us one by one.

"There you are," she said. "You've come back, finally. I'm so glad to see all of you."

Maya was evidently under the impression that I knew what the hell was going on because she didn't make a move herself or seem inclined to offer any introductions or explanations. She had that glass of rum in her lap. The ice was just as I had seen it last.

Then, suddenly, the woman seemed to remember herself. "My God," she said, "how clumsy of me." She came over and began kissing our cheeks, calling us by name. She didn't hesitate over any of them. She said something in French to Rami, a pleasantry that called for a set response, which he offered in return, diplomatically. In English, the woman had an accent, though not an especially strong one. I wondered if it was genuine. She wasn't very tall but carried herself as though she were a larger, more formidable figure. On her cheeks was a blush, maybe from the sun or from the wind.

"I'm so sorry," she said, "when you came in, I was . . ."

She didn't finish the thought. A wave of the hand did it for her. What did it mean? She went on like this, in a way that suggested and then imposed a sort of sympathy, or an understanding. Bruce had invited her, evidently. They were—here she hesitated over the word just long enough to make you question what it really meant—colleagues.

"For his new book," she said. "A little project. He suggested we get ahead of it."

Get ahead of it? Of what? And yet, it made a certain kind of sense. I even had a vague memory of him having mentioned it. I had agreed, perhaps, that it would be a good idea. I was eager for him to come, and ready to make any compromise.

Her name was Camille. No last name was offered. She was French, I gathered.

Bruce had given her the directions. He had drawn a little map, which she showed us. It wasn't an easy place to find without a map. A GPS would lead you into marshland. At night, sometimes we would see headlights: people who were lost there.

Evidently, he hadn't told her about his leaving. She didn't seem bothered by it.

"Writers," she said. "If only one of them could keep an appointment book, there would be no stopping them. They'd take over the world and bore the rest of us to tears forever."

We spent an hour, then, getting to know her, this stranger who had shown up almost as mysteriously as Bruce had gone. Apparently, she was a professor of something or other. They had met at a linguistics conference in Tours, a small academic city southwest of Paris, a two-hour drive, maybe three. What was Bruce doing in France? It seemed beside the point. At some moment in their acquaintance, Bruce had proposed that she help him prepare his notes for a new novel. It was going to be something quite different, she said.

"What do you mean by different?" I asked. "Aren't they meant to follow a formula?"

"Yes, of course," she said. "All narratives have a formula."

"The world has to be saved, I mean."

"Saved?"

She seemed genuinely confused, and I let the matter go, feeling foolish, having raised it.

Whatever the precise relationship she and Bruce had struck up, he had briefed her well. She knew all about us: about Shannon and Maya's progress through the second trimester and Rami's recent work in Budapest. She asked after some people in New Haven, and Valentina seemed to know who she meant or was pretending to, to be polite.

She asked a few questions about the house, too, and I did my best to answer them.

"How about a tour?" she said. "I'm dying to see it."

The original builder, I told her, was a man named Brunson. The crew was mostly Portuguese. The architect had a modest reputation, having designed grander homes in Newport when he was young. There were a few odds and ends lying around, antiques.

It was rather pleasant, walking beside her. She wore perfume, something with citrus notes. Valentina almost never wore perfume because it might trigger a migraine. When I was younger, I had developed a cheap fondness for women's scents and occasionally found myself brought under their sway, moved to dreamy, unknown places, making a lot of connections and suppositions that had no basis but within my own distorted reality. Now, I tried merely to enjoy a scent as I came across it: a simple pleasure, a curiosity. Marriage teaches you these things: how to compromise, what to keep private.

As we passed the harpoon, which I had finally mounted, she stopped to look closer.

"May I?"

I took it down and handed it to her. She gripped it roughly, like a sailor might.

"Yes," she said. "I've seen them before."

"Where?"

"My father collected."

"Harpoons?"

"Oh, this and that."

I thought she might go on, but she merely studied the harpoon and pursed her lips.

"It's so perfect," she said. "In its own way, a perfect object."

She was feeling its weight, leaning back, testing how it would be to throw the thing.

Maya called out from the living room. She had poured me a drink. I didn't remember asking for one, but she seemed to think I had. It was rum, like the one she was drinking.

It was then, finally, that I remembered to ask about the kids. It should have been the first place my mind went, coming home like that after a night out and a walk on the beach, after finding a stranger on my sofa. Somehow it hadn't occurred to me sooner.

"They're wonderful," Camille said. "Remarkable, those two. Twins almost always are."

"You met them?"

"Of course. I'm afraid I interrupted their movie. They were very decent about it."

Maya began apologizing. She had let them stay up late. "It was that movie," she said.

"Christ, that movie," Valentina said. "They'd die watching it. Ecstatic, happy to go."

I didn't know what movie they were talking about. The twins had a rather obsessive streak. It was impossible to keep track of whatever had grabbed their attention in a week. That was something they got from their mother. When they were engaged with something, an activity or idea, it was like the world around them would simply vanish.

"How late were they up?" I asked.

Camille was the one who answered. "Oh, not so late," she said. "Don't worry. Children are so much more resilient than we understand. And yet we say so all the time, don't we? Reassure ourselves about their sturdiness. But it's more true than we'll ever know."

What did that mean? Ten-thirty, eleven? Maya mouthed something: an apology, maybe.

I asked Camille whether she had children. It seemed the polite question, the obvious one. She smiled as she had before, indulgently, and like it was a very forward thing to ask, despite the speech she had just delivered, which sounded almost prepared, and which had annoyed me, although there was really nothing special about it to object to.

"Yes," she said. "And twins, if you can imagine. A boy and a girl."

"How old?"

"Oh, older all the time. They shock you that way, too, don't they?"

She sounded wistful about them, and I imagined they were older, perhaps off living enviably in Paris or some other city, pursuing their education but only in a lighthearted manner. Something in the way she had breezed into our lives told me she would have raised her children that way, even if she was an academic who went to conferences in Tours and struck up odd, useful relationships with American novelists.

And yet, how old was she? I thought she might be the same age as the rest of us, give or take a few years, but the closer I looked, the less sure I felt.

She stood then and stretched. And a yawn, a rather loud one.

"I'll admit," she said. "I'm quite tired. I'm wondering if . . ."

Valentina asked me to show her to her room: She must be exhausted, traveling all day.

I felt at a loss. It might have occurred to me before that she was staying with us, in the house, but I hadn't thought the matter through. I certainly hadn't considered which room to put her in. Valentina enjoyed watching me squirm and let it linger for a moment.

Then she put it to Camille. "Are you and Bruce bunking up?"

Bunking up was the expression she used: like we were all at sleepaway camp.

"Oh, I think not," Camille said. "Anyhow, he's not here, is he? Not tonight."

We put her upstairs, two doors down from the twins. There was a rather small bathroom beside her, though the floorboards in that stretch of hall creaked like a banshee and there was no going anywhere, day or night, with any kind of discretion.

She said how kind we all were. Just as she'd known we would be. She must have repeated that three or four times, so that it sounded almost like she was making a joke.

n bed that night, Valentina wanted to hear what I thought. She wanted me to speak first.

I told her I didn't know. I didn't know what to make of any of it. I was feeling drunk.

That made her laugh. It always made her laugh when I lost control in small ways.

"I think Rami's going to jump her if Bruce doesn't hurry up, get his ass back here," she said. "I could smell it on him, couldn't you? Or her. That hint of salt. A tide coming in. Something crass beneath the elegant exterior. Men will go crazy for that kind of thing."

"How old do you think she is?" I asked.

"It doesn't matter. Late twenties, probably."

"You can't be serious. She's older than that. Older than us, don't you think?"

"Older? No. God, you're bad at that. Imagine if you were ever on the witness stand."

"I'm only curious. I couldn't . . . I couldn't get a read on her."

"Didn't Bruce tell you she was coming?"

I hesitated. "Yes, I think so. He must have. Did he mention anything to you?"

"You must think she's attractive. You always pretend to have questions when you think a woman's attractive. Remember that time I caught you looking over the fence at that Gardezy girl, home for the break? And you asked me, what? Whether she was blind?"

"She was wearing dark glasses."

"She was sunbathing."

"I thought I saw a cane beside her."

"Was that it, a cane?"

She was enjoying the memory, the joke, all over again.

"I'm just wondering why she's here," I said. "It's a fair question."

The laughter dried up. "To help him on a novel. That's what they're calling it."

"How long do you think she'll stay?"

"I don't know. She seemed interesting. I'm glad she's here. Sometimes I get tired of being the only one who wasn't in that dorm of yours. It's nice to have another outsider."

I paused. Maybe too long. Or it was what she wanted.

"But you're not an outsider," I said, rather weakly.

She was smiling to herself, thinking about something. I had to ask her what it was.

"What do you think would have happened if we had met earlier?" she asked. "When you met all of them. I think about that sometimes. There were so many contingencies."

I thought the question over for a moment. She seemed to really want to know.

"You would have gotten bored of me," I said.

"Were you boring then?"

"Sometimes, yes. Were you?"

"I tried not to be. I spent all my time trying not to be boring. It was an illness."

It felt like a discussion we had had before. Like we were using the very same words, even. That happens sometimes in relationships, and you have to learn that it's natural.

She grew quite serious and asked whether I ever imagined, when we were in bed, that she was still the age she was when we met. If I ever thought about the first times we were together and tried to fuck her that way again? That was a common desire, she said, one that kept many couples together, in fact, and interested. They could imagine each other as they had been. In the same way, we passed a mirror and saw ourselves young. There was a continuity to our most intimate memories. Nothing really changed.

"That means," she said, "you're always, or often, fucking the twenty-nine-year-old me."

She had taken hold of my hand in the midst of this lecture. She pressed it down between her legs. Once, she had done that and had challenged me to remove it, but I couldn't. Or maybe I could have but was sure that in the process I would have hurt her.

"But I was already learning to be boring then," she said. "At twenty-nine I was forcing myself to be that way, sometimes. It's how you get by, how you learn. At twenty-five, you wouldn't have known what to do with me. At nineteen, neither of us would have known, and it would have been a disaster. It would have ended quickly and very badly."

"At nineteen," I said, "you wouldn't have given me a second look."

She moved on top of me and pretended to be studying me closely. She ran her hand along my cheek. It wasn't a pitying gesture. It was more like she was initiating an exam.

"Let's fuck like we're strangers," she said. "Like I've just appeared on your doorstep."

"But how old are we?"

"Just this old." She leaned back, proud, showing herself off.

I pressed her against the headboard again. Pinned her arms back, trying to remember what it was like our first time together, after we finished three bottles of wine at a place on Lafayette Street, then made out against the scaffolding in front of a church that was being restored. A woman who was walking her dog passed by toward the start of it. Then, forty, fifty minutes later, she was headed home from the park and saw we were still there, still pressed against the plywood wall, and said, rather offhand, not especially caring whether she was heard or acknowledged, "Why don't you go home if that's how you feel about it?"

We did go home, we must have. To her apartment, I think. She lived in Manhattan, so it would have been easier. But all I could remember was how it felt on the street. The rest of the night was entirely gone from memory. Like it was erased. The memory of it, collapsing into itself. Did we find a taxi, or did we walk? All I had was the start of it.

When we were finished, she snuck down the hall to clean up and came back into the room looking as though she were surprised to find me there. Had she really imagined we were strangers? Probably she had. She could tell herself just what to imagine and then do it. Her resolve was that strong and the spell would take some time to wear off.

"You always look so proud afterward," she said. "Like a peacock with its feathers out."

"The feathers are what they use to get all that," I said. "After, they put them away."

"What do you know about peacocks?"

She was right, of course. I didn't know a thing. I was only guessing.

I asked whether they had many peacocks in Venezuela.

"We have guacamayas. In the city, they come to sunbathe on the balconies."

"Those are macaws?"

Again, it was a conversation we had had before. It was all familiar.

"Yes, but macaw is an ugly word."

I repeated the Spanish, guacamaya, and asked what other birds they had in the capital, but by then she was asleep. It wasn't an act. She could fall asleep like that, in a moment.

'd like to think we were a naturally welcoming group, occasional fits of wariness or intransigence aside. Camille was easy to accommodate in those first days. She asked for nothing much and seemed always to be engaged in the resolution of some private concern that would nevertheless be given up at a moment's notice in favor of other suggestions: a swim, a project, another round of drinks. Also, she took lunch quite seriously, as the rest of us did, and never said anything about the green wine. I kept expecting her to, but her manners were too good for that, or else she really didn't care.

By the third or fourth day after her arrival, you would have thought she was just another old friend. There was hardly any further discussion about when Bruce was coming back or where he had gone off to. It would have seemed rude, like an admission that we hadn't simply invited her around in the first place, in her own right.

Soon, she began using the desk downstairs, in the garden room. Mornings, she would bring down a canvas bag filled with papers and work without interruption for two hours, then come out to join the rest of us, whatever we happened to be doing, never mentioning what she was up to or saying anything proud or put upon that might suggest she was holding our leisure against us. It wasn't fair to draw those kinds of comparisons to Bruce, especially under the circumstances, but it was almost impossible not to, knowing she was down there, working at that desk, in a room we set up for him.

I heard Valentina ask her once about the noise, whether it wasn't a bother in the mornings. She was trying to find out if Bruce had really been able to hear us that day he had claimed he could, when we kept him from writing. Camille said it was perfectly tranquil in there, she couldn't hear a thing: What should she be listening for, anyway? Something sly or coy like that, which you really couldn't decipher one way or the other.

It caught me somewhat off guard one morning when I was planning to walk into town and she asked if she might come along. She wanted to know where the library was. I told her I didn't think she would find many linguistics texts, not in the village, anyway.

"That's all right," she said. "Linguistics isn't my subject."

I had thought it was. Hadn't she and Bruce met at a conference?

"Oh yes," she said. "But I wasn't there to deliver a paper. It was at this chateau in the valley. An old house, which nobody cares about until it's time to hold a conference. They have them all over the region. A place to catch a cold in the middle of summer."

She seemed to think that explained the matter. I felt suddenly odd walking beside her. I was barefoot, for one thing, and dragging behind me the kids' beat-up red wagon, empty except for the sneakers I would need to go inside the package store. She took off her shoes, too, and put them in the wagon beside mine as though it were a local custom.

We went on that way, barefoot, for the length of the road, which ran beside a salt pond.

She was a historian, as it turned out. I was embarrassed, not having asked about it before, but figured maybe that was her preference. Europeans are always going on about Americans asking immediately what a person does for a living rather than waiting to find out, or never knowing, simply taking acquaintances as they find them.

"I have an appointment," she said. "At half past eleven. I hope I can still make it."

She looked at her wrist, expecting to find a watch there.

"I'm going to see some photographs," she said. "The library has a collection."

"A collection of what?"

"Ghosts. Marginalia, mostly. Diaries, plans, photographs from the Spiritualist camp."

She had a way of answering that suggested something was askew in the question.

"So that's your subject," I said. "You're a historian of the supernatural?"

"At the moment I'm studying their social movements. Why? Don't you believe?"

"Do you?"

Another flash of something unexpected, teasing, but no answer.

The library was nearby the package store, but she only wanted to be pointed in the right direction. She said it was important that she learn her own way, so I left her on the corner of Huckleberry and Shaw and had to chase her down from twenty yards off to give back the shoes she had left in the wagon. She didn't thank me and for some reason I wasn't expecting her to. It was altogether an uncanny but not unpleasant exchange, and as I went about my shopping and filling up the wagon with the wine and liquor we'd need for the week ahead, I found myself thinking about her and wishing I had asked to go along. The library was a small, shingled building with a good air conditioner that was always running full tilt. It was like walking into a movie theater.

Was she really in her twenties? I didn't think so but trusted Valentina's guess better than my own. In any case, what did it matter? She would get bored of us on her own schedule. Except it's never fun being the ones left behind when someone has had enough.

———○———

Later, two or three hours after, maybe more, I saw her at the end of Water Street looking at the options the intersection presented and not appearing too convinced by any of them. I flagged her down. I had killed time in town for no particular reason, just wandering around the center for the afternoon, finding things to do. I had sat for a while on the pier and watched the ferry come and go. A man in a dinghy was selling mussels and razor clams. I bought a bushel of each, then had to find ice to cool them on.

She didn't seem surprised to see me again.

"Am I on the right track?" she asked. "I don't feel that I am, but there's no telling."

She was looking for the old campground, where the photographs had been taken.

There hadn't been Spiritualists around in a hundred years. Once, the town had been busy with them. They came from all over New England. The camp wasn't very well marked, so I offered to show her the way, unless she preferred figuring it out alone.

"Some of your family," she said. "They belonged, didn't they?"

"Yes," I said. "Vaguely."

"The collection is wonderful. You wouldn't believe the things they got up to."

"Séances, communications, ritual baths. Double-exposed photographs, sometimes."

"So you're familiar?"

"Was there more to it than that? I always took it for a hobby. An eccentricity."

"Is that what they taught you in school? You did go to school here, didn't you?"

"For a semester only. Before that, I would visit for the summer."

"This was after your parents . . . ?" She trailed off, as people usually did.

"I needed a guardian," I said. "My aunts stepped in."

"It must have been a very lonely time. But perhaps the summers were more lively?"

It felt suddenly like I was being deposed. The truth is, I never had that combative spirit lawyers are meant to possess. If I talked myself into circles or contradictions, it was usually because I wanted things to be agreeable. I wanted people simply to carry along.

The campground was a half mile outside the center, on some high ground that overlooked the harbor. The land was purchased from a Wampanoag group that kept a fishing retreat nearby. The first Spiritualists had come down from Boston in the 1890s with a certain belle epoque whimsy that cost them three of four false starts when trying to build structures that would house their lot even through the mild summer months. By the turn of the century, give or take, they found a decent carpenter to build them a few cabins. A group of about fifty or sixty used to come down from the city starting in June.

The coastal land was believed to have a special wavelength or disposition that would help lure in the ghosts they were trying to summon and communicate with. This went on every summer for a decade or two, until they gave it up. The cabins were still around. They appeared somewhat artificial, something a tourist board would concoct after the fact. To my knowledge, the town had never really tried to make any money off them. You never heard much about the town's origins, in fact. When you did, the history tended to focus on the fishing fleet, which began soon after the Spiritualists left.

And yet, there were remnants of the movement all around, still. The village itself was laid out in a manner that was supposed to be pleasing to visitors from the other realm. There were no road grids and hardly any straight lines. The ghosts were thought to appreciate rounder edges. Little touches like that. The parklands had been preserved too. They had once been meeting grounds. At its peak, the camp drew in a few thousand. Some were day-trippers from Boston, and others stayed through the season.

I asked Camille how it all fit into her research. What, exactly, was she looking for?

"I study communal movements," she said. "I started in utopianists, postrevolutionary, mostly focused on the northeastern states, middle- and late-nineteenth century, then branched out. The Spiritualists were Christians. People don't always understand that. They assume they're related somehow to occultists we know today, fortune tellers, all that spectacle. But they weren't charlatans. Some were, but that wasn't the foundation."

We had made our way down a dirt path that crossed the dry land beside a salt marsh. She was looking inside one of the cabins, studying it the way you might if you had a particular purpose for the space and were concerned whether it would prove suitable.

"They were also products of the Enlightenment," she said. "In an optimistic fashion. Like most of what was going on in America in those days, especially the Northeast. Small, hopeful offshoots, everywhere you looked. They had an enduring faith in science, as well as the rest. Many of them thought the new sciences, the advances, would prove them out eventually. Perhaps that's why they took so many photographs."

At the center of the camp was a wooden structure called the wigwam. Camille ran a hand along one face, feeling the wood. The roof was round at the base and came to a sharp point at the top, giving the structure an overall impression of a rather jaunty hat.

"They claimed Native spirits told them to build it like this," she said. "They insisted they were working off precise plans but never produced any, except ones they drew up themselves. But they were quite sincere about it. What you have to remember is that these were ordinary people from Boston. Businessmen, mostly. Very bourgeois, buttoned up, but a fire had overtaken them. A passion for something else, something that hadn't been possible, until then. Even still, they didn't know quite what it was, what to do to get it, so they went around taking dictation from the local spirits."

The building only faintly resembled a wigwam. There was something grotesque about it, whereas the Indigenous architecture in the region had always struck me as so well proportioned.

I asked her what it had to do with Bruce's new novel. Was he writing about ghosts?

She seemed to find the suggestion preposterous.

"He wanted to write something serious," she said. "More honest, is my suspicion."

"Is that what you're here for? To help him be more serious?"

"Me? God, no. I think he was hoping to fuck me, don't you? One can only presume."

We walked a little farther into the campground. It had a strange feeling to it, that space. On the one hand it was a small clearing. But it was also something else, and there was no good reason why it should have been preserved except it inspired that murky sensation, that feeling of wasteful exuberance: a notion that had run its course in vain.

"The night we met," Camille said. "Did I tell you about it already?"

I gathered she was talking about Bruce again. We had been silent for some time.

"At the conference," I said. "In a chateau, outside Tours. In the valley."

"Are you making fun of me?"

"Not at all."

"Do you know the area?"

I shook my head. She seemed satisfied or was simply eager to tell her story.

"I was at the bar," she said. "Alone and overcome. There had been a dreary lecture. Everyone was under its influence still, but I was experiencing something different and Bruce . . . he had a way of picking you out. He must have noticed me then and came over to see what the matter was. He spoke to me in German at first. I didn't know why."

I could imagine why but didn't think it my place to interrupt.

We were standing near an outbuilding that appeared to have been a bathhouse once.

"I was experiencing this intense feeling," she said. "Not of nostalgia, but something close to it. You see, when I was very young, I was given a dollhouse. An extravagant thing. A gift from one of my aunts who hadn't children of her own. It was the kind of toy my parents disapproved of. They thought girls were corrupted by dollhouses. By gifts, for that matter. They wanted me to be very serious and concerned with other people, with the world and not with myself. But a gift is a gift, so what to do? I kept it. It took up nearly an entire room, a maid's chamber nobody used. For about a year, I played with it obsessively. Every day, for hours on end. A little family lived inside the house, and I would impose dramas on them. Scandals and such. Sometimes, they would fight and become estranged for a time, so I would keep them in separate rooms."

She paused, and this time I said something. I said it sounded like she was rather lonely.

She was shielding her eyes from the sun. She was sweating quite a lot.

"Yes," she said. "Lonely, intensely so. Do you know what happened then to the dollhouse? I lost interest. It had consumed me, and then nothing, I felt nothing for it."

"Kids grow up," I said. "That's how it goes. The twins are like that too."

The sweat was pooling around her collarbone.

"Yes, I saw that. They really are remarkable children. Did I tell you that already?"

"You did."

"Well, I lost interest in my toy. Years went by, decades. I hadn't thought of it, even once, until that night, arriving at the conference, when I saw the chateau, what it was: the very same structure. My dollhouse must have been built as a replica from its design. Nobody ever told me it was a replica. I simply discovered it, by chance. I was quite moved to be inside it. Frightened too. Sitting alone at the bar, among all those silly academics, with my very confused memories. And that was how Bruce found me. Speaking to me in German. Asking was I all right. Did I want company? And hearing him, I was startled again, more so. Because . . . and here, I know this sounds foolish . . . it was because the family, the one living in my dollhouse, who I would invent stories about, were German also. Why should a small girl want her dolls speaking German?"

"I don't know."

"But you agree, it's quite odd? A potent series of coincidences."

She seemed to really want to know the answer. I agreed, it was odd, all of it.

"That was it," she said. "That was how I met your friend."

Had they gone to bed that night at the chateau? I found myself wondering about it as we carried on our inspection of the campground. It wasn't a very kind thing to be thinking about, and yet natural enough, especially in that space, the campground, which had little of interest to see and yet was equal portions ridiculous and suggestive.

I kept thinking she would tell more of the story, but she kept at a distance. She was circling the bathhouse structure, and I got the feeling she was considering going inside. To do what? There was nothing for her in there—no running water, no relief—and yet it really did seem that was what she was thinking about doing. Or was I letting my mind get away from me? It felt like we were the only two people around for a great distance, though in fact the village center was nearby, and if you cut through the woods, back toward the road, you would within ten minutes or so emerge behind a Dunkin' Donuts.

———○———

Later, as we were walking home, she asked if we might stop. The sun was getting to be too much. It was a hot day and there hadn't been any cloud cover since early that morning. That was why the library had seemed so appealing, probably, and why I regretted not going with her. We were making our way along the salt pond's bank, about a half mile from the house. I pointed out a shady elm tree where we could pause.

From the bank you could make out, just over the tree line, two of the house's gables.

"It's such a lovely home," she said.

I was glad she thought so. I was always hungry for those compliments.

"I saw photographs," she said. "At the library. A series of the house's construction. I was thinking, it's interesting you didn't mention it before. On that first night, for example, when you were giving me a tour. If it were my house and it had been built for that purpose, it would be the first thing I would tell everyone. Then again, before, when I asked whether your family was involved in the movement, you said only vaguely, as though it were something you weren't quite accustomed to speaking about."

"I didn't know it was your field, or I would have said more."

"So it was modesty, that's all?"

The history of it was all so eccentric, it was hard to take seriously. The house was originally intended as the Spiritualist community's first year-round foothold in the town—a place where they could spend the winter, essentially. It was my great-great-grandmother who was dedicated to the project, who had been quite taken in by the group's beliefs and persuaded to commit some portion of the family's resources to supernatural expeditions, as they were sometimes called. She had lost her three sons—two in war, another to disease; some kind of flu—and spent the rest of her life trying to speak to them. It wasn't so unusual for the period. People died all the time, wantonly. Any number of religions and movements were formed to help make sense of it or to prove that it wasn't really happening at all: It was only a matter of spirits crossing over.

By the time the house was finished, my ancestor had crossed over herself. She hadn't remembered to make any special accommodations for her fellow believers in the will, and the property was passed down in the ordinary course, a little large for its new purposes but nonetheless appreciated. The community had mostly disbanded by then. Some of the old families stayed on and were integrated into the town. They opened hotels or bought an interest in a fishing boat. They tried on new religions, new enterprises, and didn't talk a great deal about what had brought them to the area to begin with. They were old New Englanders, accustomed to suppressing such matters.

I didn't mention any of this to Camille. I got the impression she knew most of it anyhow. She was a historian, after all, and had gone to inspect the library's collection.

In all likelihood, she knew a great deal more about it than I did.

"Your aunts," she said, "the ones who took you in. They lived here all their lives?"

"My aunt Louisa did," I said. "She grew up in the house. Eileen was her partner."

"They were queer?"

"A Boston marriage, it was called."

"Of course. I've always liked that term. Do you know for years I would see it in the material, diaries, but never knew what it meant? Sometimes a euphemism eludes you, like a language. Then the logic is suddenly clear. I felt so stupid once I understood it."

How many years? I wondered. Perhaps in France they started their research earlier.

"And where were you married?" she asked.

The question struck me as rather abrupt. Purposefully so.

I told her about the barroom ceremony in New York. It was one of those memories I had put to words so many times before, now it felt as though there was only one manner of recounting the event. I mentioned the pulpit, the wood stove, and the speeches my friends gave. Then, how Valentina's relatives were unable to attend.

"Valentina is very beautiful," she said. "In a way that must feel burdensome at times."

"That's an odd observation."

"Is it? I try to say things that strike me as interesting. I was wondering, trying to put myself in her shoes, what she makes of your friends. She must have a favorite of them."

"A favorite?"

"I can see how they respond to her. How they crave her attention."

I thought about it for a time, taking the question seriously.

"Rami," I said. "She's always felt a bond with him."

"But she met you first?"

"I don't mean in that way."

"What other way is there? Attraction is a matter of degrees, not kind, don't you think?"

"Not especially. There's eros and then . . . the others."

"Yes, the others." She smiled but seemed unpersuaded. "And what of Bruce? You two share a strong resemblance. I don't suppose I'm the first one ever to notice. Did you ever compete for girls? I imagine he was quite awkward when he was younger. Trying on all those personalities, those affects, and so unsure which would suit him best."

"You picked up all that at the conference in Tours?"

"That was only our first meeting. And we've corresponded, quite a lot."

I realized then that she had been studying us. She had developed her theories and was eager to try them out. I was her sounding board. Or there was something else going on.

She looked at me quite carefully. "I have a confession."

She was waiting for something: for me to ask her to make it, maybe.

I noticed she wasn't sweating any longer. She seemed quite placid.

"The first night," she said. "When I arrived here, something struck me. An idea."

"What idea?"

"Well, you were showing me the house. Do you remember?"

She had only just mentioned it: the tour, and the details I had left out. Of course I did.

"I don't mean to say it was a premonition, that would be too strong. Another coincidence, really. As we were walking down that long hallway, after you showed me the harpoon, an idea came to me. I thought: They've done away with Bruce. They're hiding it from me."

"Hiding what?" I asked.

"The body. The fact of it."

"That's absurd."

She smiled now. "But in the moment, I became convinced. I was terrified but quite curious too. Curious to see how you would manage it. How you would distract and charm me and find a way to make me leave before I discovered what had happened. All this occurred to me, really, in a moment. The way an idea takes hold, then vanishes."

"And now you think it was something else."

"It was the house: a house built for ghosts. I must have sensed that."

"Except the ghosts never came. The house wasn't finished in time."

"Sad, isn't it? But our intentions linger sometimes. Is that absurd, too, do you think?"

I thought it over for a while before answering. "Not absurd, no."

A mass of clouds came in and we left our shelter. It felt as though we had been there for a great deal of time. The whole afternoon was that way: strangely elongated or bent.

At some point on the way, she stopped and pointed at a bird that was circling the pond. It was one of the ospreys that lived nearby in the marsh. There was no mistaking that wingspan, even at a distance. The osprey gave the area its name. The colonists took them for buzzards because of their enormous size, though in fact they're raptors and carry on accordingly, like hawks. She said something about wanting to see how it fished.

A moment later, as though the bird had received a signal, it began to dive. Watching an osprey dive that way is rather alarming if it's your first experience. There comes a point when you're certain a crash is coming, that it's going to be tremendous, ruinous. Then the bird tilts its body a few degrees and enters the water with its talons out and its wings tucked. How they can spot the fish that far off, and track them at such a murderous speed, is one of nature's bloody marvels. Locally, the birds were revered. There was a customary belief, passed down through generations, which I heard repeated many times, that the birds used some kind of trick of movement that persuaded the fish, once targeted, to turn their bellies to the surface and to give themselves willingly over to the talons. The idea being that the bird and the fish are united in that moment, somehow, and that both desire the same result, however violent it may appear from outside.

The osprey came up with a fish in its grip. A shad, maybe. Its belly had been pierced.

Neither of us spoke during this time. We just watched the hunt through to the end, then carried on walking toward the house. It was a beautiful moment, in its way, and finished too soon. I had taken my shoes off again. I always walked that dirt path barefoot. When the bird went into the water, I felt my toes clench, as though it were me.

When it was finished, or sometime after, she said, "I think maybe he's dead, though."

I didn't answer her. She hadn't asked a question. At first, I thought she meant the fish.

"Bruce," she said. "Anything could have happened to him, really, don't you think? He could have been carried off by a bird. If you got a bird big enough, it could snatch him."

It was such a crazy thing to say, I couldn't help but laugh.

And yet she appeared altogether serious. More serious than she had all afternoon.

"He'd be very glad to know we're talking about him," I said.

The comment drew her back. All that seriousness, gone in an instant.

She said yes, she supposed he was conceited and given to fits of drama. "But it's just that you mean so much to him. All of this means so much to him. And you, especially. You're his best friend. He talked

about you, you know? That night at the chateau, he told me all about
you. His best friend, how it had been too long since he had seen you."

"He said that?"

She hesitated. "Yes."

"Did he really?"

After another pause, she said, "In German. You remember? We
spoke in German."

15

The others must have known about her specialty, or some part of it. Nobody seemed particularly surprised when she proposed that we hold a séance. One morning she came out from the garden room as we were setting the table for lunch and made the suggestion as though we had all been discussing that very subject. We might hold it at the house, she said, that very night if we liked. It would be simple to arrange with a few phone calls. I was holding on to a salad bowl as she spoke, and for some reason, the size of the bowl seemed extravagantly overgrown, like it had swollen out of proportion. I wanted to put it down but the table was already too crowded with plates.

"But why would we do that?" I asked.

"To test the house," she said. "Aren't you curious what it's capable of?"

She didn't seem at all serious about it. There was an appeal to that kind of lightness.

She said she would try Miss Huxley as soon as the library opened. Miss Huxley was an archivist connected to the library's Spiritualist collection. Also, evidently, a self-appointed medium, someone Camille had already been in touch with.

There was a consensus in favor, and I soon gave over to it. We were in that stretch of summer when almost any diversion gets a warm welcome. Within an hour, we were all busy with preparations, touches that would make the place more suitable.

I remembered there was a set of kerosene lanterns in the shed. Shannon helped me get them working and laid out, while Rami undertook the assembly of a rather august three-part jerry-rigged table that could fit the six of us, plus Miss Huxley, with leftover spaces for equipment, as well as any spectral guests. This was in the living room. (There had been some discussion about the best location for it, but ultimately the living room won out.) Valentina and Maya went around hanging sheets over the windows wherever the curtains and shades weren't strong enough to keep out the light. It was odd, watching the house transform. I liked to believe that the way we had it arranged had an inevitable logic, yet it looked quite natural done up in Victorian style.

Camille was the final arbiter on all this. She seemed to know what was needed and what could be done without. But I got the feeling she was putting us on in some fashion, or like she was only trying to be accommodating, having sensed the slight malaise settling in about the group and wanting to give us this thing, this evening, all together, and for it all to come off well. Why she should care or why a séance, of all things, was what we needed, I didn't know.

After dinner, we cleared the table and put away the wine. Camille said we wouldn't want alcohol around. The experience shouldn't be clouded in any manner, apparently.

We were waiting only on Miss Huxley, whom we had been told to expect sometime around nightfall, or just before, because she didn't much care for the idea of driving the dirt roads alone at night. I was still feeling some ambivalence toward the evening and went down to the beach in order to throw rocks at the waves, when I saw that Rami had beat me to it. He was there, wearing his green holiday shorts, but on top was a button-down shirt with a stiff collar. I thought it was rather sweet of him to dig it out for the occasion. It must have been one of his work shirts, perhaps something he had worn in Budapest.

"Are you thinking about a swim?" I asked, for want of anything to say, and sensing that he was working through some apprehension of his own.

"What time do you think we'll start?" he asked.

"Soon, I guess. Why, got plans for later?"

He checked his wrist. It was nearly the same gesture I had seen from Camille when we were walking to the library and she was talking about her appointment. An ordinary gesture, yes, but the way they both executed it seemed somehow practiced—coordinated.

I wondered if they had slept together. Valentina was sure they would, sooner or later.

"I've never done anything like this before," he said.

"Neither have I. I guess that's why she proposed it."

"She has a charisma about her. Have you noticed?"

"Is that what it's called?"

"It's easy to get swept up in her enthusiasm."

I suddenly wondered if we were talking about Camille or about somebody else.

He bent over to pick up a stone, but it didn't suit him. He must have been looking to skip them. When I had come down, I was only thinking about throwing them, but of course he was right. If you're feeling disoriented like that, skipping is always better, especially in choppy water. The wind was blowing toward the shore, but the tide was going out and you could see the currents drawing everything north toward the marsh.

He turned his back on the water and looked at the house.

"So that's really what it was for?" he asked. "They were going to do these things here?"

"I think they just wanted somewhere dry to sleep. A place to lock up the jewelry. The meetings, the events, they were mostly held around the bluffs or down on the beach. They had this wigwam. I assume that's where a lot of it went on. I don't really know."

"But did they ever get around to it? I mean, do you know whether anyone's done this sort of thing before, here in the house? It would be good to know whether they had, before we try, just to be sure what we're getting into. That probably sounds a bit ridiculous, doesn't it? It's just that I feel like I don't really understand what we're getting into."

I told him what I knew about my family, the house, all of it. Repeating the broad strokes, it sounded like a story you might tell in order to obfuscate another, less easily relayed version of events. Feeling, perhaps, I owed him something more grounded, less euphemistic, I told him, too, about a summer when I was young and my mother was asked to light flares along the harbor beach. It was part of a ceremony called Illumination Night, which was handed down from the Spiritualist days. The flares were red, meant to serve as beacons for any spirits circling the area and considering whether to visit. They didn't signify all that any longer, but that was how it had started, a century before, and my mother was chosen as torchbearer that summer. A family prerogative, maybe. She asked me along, but in the end she couldn't do it. Something about the lights frightened her. She said it was all too monstrous and handed the torch to somebody else, one of her cousins who didn't share her compunctions and got the things going, one after another. We walked home along the bluffs, I recalled, and my mother told me not to turn, not to look back. But the sky around us already appeared red, and you didn't have to look back toward the beach to see it. I was trying to remember all those details and recount them to him very accurately.

But it was coming out wrong. I wasn't seeing it clearly enough, not quite.

I was young that summer. Eight years old, still viewing things as a child does.

In any case, he didn't seem to be listening. His concern was elsewhere. I knew him well enough to know that he was hoping to get me talking only in order to soothe himself with the sound of it. That was something diplomats did, or maybe it was his own quirk.

"What is it?" I asked. "What's bothering you? Something you want to talk about?"

He took his time deciding whether it was.

"Do you know who they contact at these things? I mean, I'm just wondering whether they target certain people, or if it's just sort of a general announcement that we're around to talk if there's anyone out there who wants to chat. Like a shortwave radio."

"I think she mentioned something about my family. My great-great-grandmother."

This seemed to give him some relief. Still, there was more he wanted to say. In the meantime, he couldn't decide whether he wanted to look at the house or the sea. It was odd to see him at a loss, even of an insignificant kind. He was struggling to find his bearings.

"There was a girl in Budapest," he said.

I waited for him to go on. When he hesitated, I told him I had assumed there was.

"Did you?" he asked. He looked glad at being anticipated, if not understood.

"There's always a girl in Budapest, isn't there?"

"For me, no. But you've always thought me ambitious."

"What happened to her?"

Here, another hesitation. It occurred to me that he in fact now had the right words for what he wanted to say, but they were in another language, and he was translating for himself, or for my sake—that is, to be more perfectly understood. I had often wished I spoke those other languages, or that I had asked him to tutor me when I was still capable of learning. My French was poor, and I had no Arabic to speak of. French and English were the languages of his education. Around the house, growing up, he spoke Arabic, and I believed that was where his mind went in moments such as these.

"We got into some trouble," he said. "These things, they happen. But never had to me."

"Trouble?"

"Pregnant, of course."

His tone had grown sharper. He must have thought it mean of me to put it to him.

I chose my next question more carefully. "But not anymore?"

He shook his head. "She went back to Berlin to take care of it. It's not the sort of thing you would do in Hungary. Well, that's not true. People do it all the time, but Germans, they go back to Germany. Wouldn't trust a Magyar surgeon with the job, is what I gather."

A light flashed across us and across the water: headlights from a car. Miss Huxley.

They would be wanting us at the house soon. I didn't point it out. He already knew.

"Well," he said. "That's all over. I could have chased her down, gone to Berlin, but I didn't. She's interesting too. Likes to hike, camp, the outdoors. She was always talking about vigorous things—you know those women? No limits to what they do, what they can accomplish. She didn't tell me what she was doing in Berlin, but I suppose I knew."

I wanted to say a word to comfort him, but the situation seemed so opaque to me. Not strange or unusual, but only like I couldn't see it for what it was. Rami put a hand on my shoulder and said something to get me moving, something about tending to our guest.

"Valentina didn't mention any of this to you?" he asked.

She hadn't even hinted at it.

He found that surprising. "I just assume these things make their way back to you."

"Sometimes they do."

"Right," he said, smiling now. "She was probably waiting for the perfect moment."

"That's marriage. You get bits and pieces. The signal is never quite clear."

"Ah, so that's what it is. A signal. I've been wondering, all this time."

He stopped short of the porch, looking suddenly concerned.

"But where are the kids?" he asked.

"Asleep," I said. "Upstairs, in their room."

"Jesus Christ, are they?" He was glancing up toward their window.

I didn't see what the matter was. "Valentina read them a chapter of *Treasure Island*."

"I thought you would have sent them away for the night."

"Because of the séance?"

"I was just assuming they wouldn't be here. Is that so crazy?"

Perhaps he was right, but then why disturb their sleep? Why put them out of home?

A voice called out from the kitchen. They were looking for us. Miss Huxley was ready.

16

iss Huxley was a woman of seventy or so well-lived years, wearing a workmanlike uniform of wide-cut jeans and a weathered chore coat, which together gave her the air not of a supernaturally attuned mystic but of a friendly neighbor who had dropped by to offer some advice on the garden. There were fine lines of dirt beneath her fingernails.

She wasn't at all what I was expecting, but then the woman was a stranger to me, though apparently she had lived in town all her life and was considered the area's foremost expert on, among other things, the brief spiritual pursuits of my various dead relatives. She was quite particular about being called Miss. She had a way of pronouncing it that made it clear she didn't want you taking any liberties in that area.

"I like her," Rami whispered to me. "I had a jacket just like that once."

She reviewed our preparations and seemed to approve, especially of the lanterns, which she asked several pointed questions about, none of which I could answer competently. I suggested instead that she should feel free to wander the house, since it was of special interest to her. She did just that, for nearly a half hour, leaving the rest of us milling in the kitchen without wine, until finally she declared herself satisfied and that we really ought to begin.

It was late, she said. Nothing to be done for it—it was what the event called for. Still, she'd rather not be driving herself home at midnight, or she might end up in the marsh.

"That marsh," she said, "doesn't drain properly."

I thought it a rather odd observation. Also, it always struck me as a rather wild, fluid place.

"It's all backed up," she said. "The ratio's off. On its way to swamp."

After looking once more over the table we had arranged in the living room, laid with the finest set of blue lace cloth I could dig out of the linen closet, Miss Huxley told us with some authority where we ought to sit. Camille was at her side. They seemed only vaguely acquainted with each other, and I thought the old woman betrayed a certain impatience with her, maybe because she had already been pestered with questions at their earlier meeting, at the library, or because Camille's interest in Miss Huxley's expertise was academic and therefore inherently skeptical. I didn't think Miss Huxley would bother herself much about skeptics, French or otherwise. It was the chore coat, maybe, that gave her that practical air.

I was asked to sit apart from my wife. It felt as though we were at a dinner party. The table was wide across, much too wide for any kind of conversation, but it offered a pleasant view, and I had always enjoyed observing Valentina from a slight remove. She had such an easy way about her. She would have made anybody comfortable, no matter the setting or circumstance. Shannon was beside her. Valentina must have thought there were some nerves involved because I noticed her touching Shannon's hand, not exactly to offer comfort, but more to share in the excitement.

They had been getting closer and closer in those weeks. It wasn't just the baby coming. There seemed to be something else between them, something enviable and mysterious.

"We'll be getting started now," Miss Huxley said. She kept her jacket on despite the stuffy room. There wasn't any pomp or prelude involved. She simply closed her eyes and launched into it, rocketing herself into some other plane where presumably we might follow, or where voices would speak through hers, if I understood the role of a medium correctly. None of it had been explained, or maybe they had talked about it while Rami and I were on the beach discussing German girls who loved the outdoors.

It was then, oddly enough, that it occurred to me what he had been frightened of. Frightened isn't the right word, but concerned about. He must have been wondering whether one of the ghosts, if we ever reached them, would spill his secrets.

It was a natural thing to think of, but it hadn't occurred to me before, on the beach, which made me wonder what others might be thinking of just then—which ghosts or memories might be arriving to mind. The kitchen light was off, and we were in near darkness. The lanterns hardly gave you anything. Miss Huxley asked us to concentrate.

Concentrate on what? She didn't say, and I again found myself thinking about my wife in younger years. I often regretted not knowing her then. I knew very little, really, about her life in Venezuela, except the few fragments she shared with me, which never seemed to arrive with any true shape or coherence. Maybe it came to mind because I knew she had lost people. A boyfriend, for example. She was seventeen and they had gone to a friend's farm and the boy had asthma and hadn't brought his inhaler, or had, but it hadn't worked. They tried taking him to the hospital. They were far out in the country, and he simply stopped breathing before they arrived. She told me about him once— only once—and I hadn't pressed her with questions, though maybe I should have. I found myself thinking of him now and again, whenever the kids were sick and would start coughing in the night. There was another as well: He had visited New Haven once, with his fiancée, a Spanish girl, and after going back to Venezuela he left the office one evening and was never seen again. He was a lawyer and had issued a report the regime didn't like. In law school, he had told Valentina that he was in love with her, and she had told him he was wrong, he misunderstood, and it was left at that.

"We must concentrate ourselves," Miss Huxley said again, though this time it sounded like she thought we were a juice or a solution. "I am beginning to encounter the voices."

I was expecting one of the lanterns to blow out. A curtain to lift. Some histrionics. But it was a subdued affair and apparently not to be rushed. Miss Huxley went quite blank and had her hands laid calmly on the table and nothing happened, and nobody spoke for what seemed a long time. Outside, you could hear the wind and the tide going out.

"I am requesting," Miss Huxley said, "the attention of Mrs. Miriam Bemelmans."

That was my great-great-grandmother. Bemelmans was her maiden name. It was considered quite eccentric at the time, the fact that she insisted on being addressed by it.

Miss Huxley had mentioned before that it was important we be solicitous and polite.

"Mrs. Bemelmans," she said. "We are friends. And family. Your Jim is here with us too."

Your Jim. Nobody that I could recall had ever referred to me that way before, as theirs.

There was no response. No effect. I glanced across the table, through the lamplight, and saw my wife looking wholly absorbed in the inquiry, as though Miriam Bemelmans might any moment emerge from the tabletop or the floorboards or the wall panels and demand an accounting of who had been added to the family, what their intentions were.

Valentina would have been equal to the task. She could have stood up to any degree of interrogation by an ancient Victorian matriarch, living or otherwise. She had true poise.

Rami, on the other hand, seemed to me rather terrified. Still thinking about the girl in Budapest. Still carrying around that shame, which was needless but then unavoidable.

Miss Huxley continued. "If any spirits who are connected to Mrs. Bemelmans would kindly pass her the message that we, her friends and her family, wish to speak with her, it would be most appreciated. We will await any manner of contact. Accept our thanks."

She went on in that imploring way for a few minutes, trying all variations and means.

When nothing came of it, she went silent for a period of time, perhaps five or six minutes, then opened her eyes, which had been shut during most of that same stretch, and announced that we had too much disbelief in our ranks. It was muddying the channels of communication. It all sounded so formal, so affected, and possibly rehearsed, and she must have seen it wasn't helping matters to be talking in that way.

"It's muddier than that marsh," she said. "We've got to clean it up or we get nowhere."

There, again, was that practical air, which accompanied the coat.

"I have an idea," Camille said.

She produced, rather slowly, as though concerning herself more with the effect than with the gesture, a man's wallet. "It's Bruce's. I found it in the desk you set up for him."

"What do you mean?" I asked.

"I found it just this morning," she said.

I told her that was impossible. I'd looked all over that room. Nothing of his was there.

"It was in the back of a drawer," she said. "Perhaps you didn't notice. A mistake."

She handed it over and I looked through the contents. It was his. His cards were there. In his license photograph, he was smiling in a big, hopeful fashion like I hadn't seen him smile in years, since we were young. Or maybe I'd never seen him smile that way.

There was also a great deal of money inside. At a glance, a thousand dollars, easily. He had always kept a lot of money at hand, even in the old days when he hadn't had much.

Some people are like that. They keep it folded up neatly, and others pack it into wads.

Bruce kept his neat. I felt quite stunned by all of it, and by the way it had been produced.

"What are you proposing?" I asked.

"A personal article," Camille said. "It always helps."

She looked to Miss Huxley who confirmed this with a nod.

"He means, what are you suggesting about Bruce?" Rami asked.

"I'm suggesting," Camille said, "that perhaps he's dead. And we could reach him."

Nobody spoke. There was simply silence.

"I told Jim all this already," she said. She sounded so calm about it. If anything, she sounded apologetic, like it was an entertaining theory she had unjustly deprived the others of, when they might have liked to hear about it, as I'd had the opportunity to do.

She described, in brief, what she thought: that there had been an accident. That was why he had vanished. He hadn't gone to visit other friends or traveled to New York.

"It's possible," she said. "And here's his wallet. Don't you think it's curious?"

On the word *curious*, her accent became so strong, I thought she had slipped into French.

There was another general silence that she apparently took for assent. So did Miss Huxley, who clasped the wallet into her hand and squeezed it a few times before starting.

What was she doing? Testing the leather? Feeling all that cash, figuring the amount?

And yet somehow it all seemed to me on the level. It was laced with sincerity, all of it.

"Bruce," Miss Huxley said, after confirming the name and being sure that was how he would like to be addressed, not by his last name or something else. "Bruce, we're all here and eager to speak with you if that meets with your approval. Your friends are here. Rami and Camille and Valentina and Shannon and Maya and me, Miss Huxley. You don't know me, Bruce, but I'm here with your friends. I'm a friend. Jim is here too."

I'd have sworn the curtains moved. Probably they did. Who knows what gusts of wind were able to sneak through? Upon discerning the movement, my first thought was that Bruce was in the room, in some fashion, and was laughing at the old woman's words. But what exactly was supposed to be funny? That we were his friends? He had told Camille exactly that. I was his best friend in the world, he had said. He hadn't any family left either.

I looked around the table again. Nobody else was reacting to the curtain.

"I don't want to do this," Maya said.

Somehow, I hadn't thought of her, or looked in her direction all evening, or suspected that if somebody were going to call the event into doubt, call an end to it, it would be her. Miss Huxley didn't appear to hear her. She was deep into the process, the summoning. So Maya repeated the words again, now more forcefully, and stood up.

"This is morbid," she said. "He's not dead. He left us, is all. He fucked off in the night."

Miss Huxley still hadn't opened her eyes or yielded her efforts.

Maya looked pointedly at Shannon. "I'm going to bed."

"I want to see what happens," Shannon said.

"What do you think is going to happen?"

"I don't know. That's the point."

"Suit yourself."

And then she left. It wasn't a scene. There was no anger in it. She was simply gone.

"Shall we continue?" Miss Huxley said.

It seemed to me every face at the table was looking in my direction.

"Sure," I said. "Maybe another try. If people want to."

Miss Huxley put in another effort, lasting a few minutes at it, then said perhaps we really ought to focus on the Bemelmans line. I could have sworn a shadow crossed her face. We didn't want to upset Miriam, she said, or have her feeling like the evening hadn't been planned with her in our hearts. I couldn't even remember what she was talking about. All thoughts of my relatives had left my mind.

Camille took the wallet, Bruce's wallet, from Miss Huxley, looked it over for a moment, then handed it to me. "Perhaps we should do something with it," she said. "I'll let you decide."

Miss Huxley began droning again, and we went on that way for another hour.

It was like being part of a play. That was how it felt, and we had to get to the end of it.

17

Later, I was standing in the kitchen with Maya. She hadn't gone to bed after all. She had only removed herself to another room in order to drink rum and wait the thing out.

She asked whether we'd had any luck in the end. When I told her no, she laughed, making me feel a little foolish for having answered so quickly, and said it wasn't too nice of the girl, pulling a trick like that on us, without warning, and without it amounting to anything. "If he had turned up," she said, "it would have been different."

She looked over the wallet, which I had brought with me, but didn't comment on it.

"She did mention it to me the other day," I said. "I thought she was joking."

"That he might be dead?"

"We were walking back from town. She said when she first got here she was scared, because it dawned on her that something might have happened—that we might have done something to him—and we were covering it up. This was on the way home from the library. She was telling me how she met Bruce at some conference. How he'd chatted her up at the bar."

I described some more of the conversation as clearly as I could. It was already fading.

Maya seemed to be listening to me very closely. It was that kind of concentration that can sometimes feel like an imposition, or even an assault, and yet I didn't think she meant anything particular by it. She was just drunk, probably on her fifth or sixth rum.

"She wants to be provocative," Maya said. "She's taken that up as her role here. She's young and sexy. We're older but not so old we can't remember what it's like to be provoked. So she comes in here with that long neck and spouts some reckless bullshit."

Yes, I agreed, pouring myself another glass of wine. She did have an awfully long neck.

"If he really were gone, dead," she said, "what would that mean? What's she going around telling? It would have been the night of the fireworks. The Fourth. You fought on the beach, and nobody saw him again. That's right, isn't it? And she seems to know that timeline. She has it all worked out. You were the last to see him, and it got violent."

"She's having some fun, sure, but I don't think it's that."

"I'm not saying you've been accused. But she wants to know what would happen."

"Happen when?"

"If you were to feel accused. If we all were. To see how we would react. Would we button up, close ranks? After all, that's what she studies, isn't it? Movements? Microsocieties? We're a curiosity to her, a specimen. And already we played the part. None of us looked into what happened to him, not really. We carried on, happy to be rid of him, if we're being honest. That's interesting. We've got the girl's attention now."

"She studies utopianists. Spiritualists. Not accomplices to murder."

"That's what all true believers are. Accomplices."

"He left us. He went back to New York."

"Or he's at a hotel."

"He's at another friend's house. Drinking their wine. Writing his book."

She shrugged, and her concentration seemed to break with the gesture.

"It was a good show," she said. "Very dramatic. And hell, she's good-looking."

"How old do you think she is?"

She didn't hear the question or didn't bother to answer. She was thinking about Camille's neck again, maybe, and about how it had looked on display in the lamplight.

"I kept expecting the phone to ring," she said. "Right in the middle of it, once she started searching for Bruce. I kept wondering, Do they still have a landline here? I was sure it would ring like that, and it would be Bruce calling to tell us we'd been shit friends or something. He'd be home in his apartment feeling bad about how it went, and his solution would be to call up, say something nasty over the phone, just at that moment."

"It would have been nice to hear his voice, anyway."

"It would have proved you hadn't killed him. That he wasn't dead after all."

"Yes, that too."

She smiled a little ruefully. "But you're not really worried."

"No."

"If he hadn't gone home, if he were missing, we would have heard from somebody."

"Who? He didn't have anybody."

"He had a book due, right? His editor might have thought it was strange not hearing from him all this time. A deadline blown could do it. Or his agent. Some woman he's fucking in the city. I don't know, maybe he has a bagel shop he goes by every morning."

"He was fucking Camille. And we've heard what she thinks."

"He was hoping to. There's a difference. He lured her here but hadn't managed it yet."

"Did she tell you that?"

"I don't need to be told, Jim. It's one of the advantages on our side."

I nodded and looked at my wineglass. I didn't want any more.

"Still, I didn't like it in there," she said. "What was going on—it was cheap. And yet I really did think the phone was going to ring just then, exactly when we were calling him, so what does that say about me? What does it say I believe? I'll believe anything."

"You're suggestible. We all are, especially when we're together."

"Like a coven."

"More like angry townsfolk, with witches to burn."

Another laugh came out, more scornful now. "Poor Mrs. Bemelmans. Miriam's just trying to enjoy herself in the afterlife. Here we are, shouting at her all fucking night. What I can never understand is why anyone would bother coming back, once they're through. If that's what it is, I'm sure there's plenty to do on the other side. You'd forget all about what was going on here, wouldn't you? You'd try. You wouldn't care about your great-great-grandson and his friends or the one of them who got his feelings hurt."

Seeing my glass was empty, she poured me a finger of rum. It was dark and very sweet.

"You know," she said, "he asked me to paint his portrait."

"Bruce did?"

She nodded. "This was two years ago, maybe. One of those summer afternoons when it feels like there's nobody left in the city and you wish it would just fucking rain already. He called me up after lunch, and it was funny because I had been thinking about him. I saw one of his books reviewed in the paper. I hadn't thought they would review him in the paper, but then, there it was. Half a page. An illustration at the top. I was thinking, that'll puff him up a bit, won't it? Not just the money, now, but there in ink too. And then that day, he calls me and asks if we can meet. He's all earnest and aw-shucks and waiting for me to ask him what it's about so he can be cute, but I just say, sure, buy me a coffee, tell me where. We meet up, somewhere far off, uptown. For half an hour he's asking me these questions about the history of portrait painting. It's obvious he's done his homework, and at first, I'm thinking it must be research for a book, his next one. Then I realize, no, this guy wants me to paint him. You can just tell with some people."

"Did you?"

"Paint him? No, I got the hell out of the café."

"But you were sure that's what he wanted."

"No doubt in my mind. He'd known just the day to call. I was thinking about him."

It was such a strange story. Such a strange idea, for Bruce to want her to paint him.

I said something to that effect, but Maya shook her head.

"It wasn't that strange," she said. "We could've used the money back then."

"But what did he want it for? Who wants a portrait of themselves?"

"People do, all the time. They don't care what you think of them, just put it in oil."

I tried imagining what she would have done. How she would have painted him.

The whole thing seemed ridiculous, and yet I had no doubt he was serious about it.

"The odd thing is," she said, "I was glad he called. Glad he asked. I loved him sometimes, and it was usually when he was an ass, like in that moment, calling me up."

There was more she was about to say, but something stopped her short.

I felt it too: that certainty you're no longer alone in a room, not as you thought you were. I looked over and saw the kids were on the stairs, watching us. They were in pajamas and their faces were pressed to the railing. The staircase dropped into the kitchen. The service stairs, my aunts used to call them. We called them the back way.

How long had they been sitting there? It was impossible to know.

"We want something to drink," one of them said. They wanted orange juice. Another time, I would have said no, it was too late, they could have water or nothing, but in that moment, I only opened the refrigerator, found what they were after, and gave it to them, as simple as that. It felt good, being able to do that for them, without any questions or haggling or looking to somebody else to make sure that it was all right.

When they had left, Maya said she had better call it a night before things got morbid again.

"That scared the hell out of me," she said. The kids showing up like that, she meant.

It was true, she really did seem unnerved. She was unsteady going up the stairs.

had forgotten to bring a glass with me to bed and woke up in the night and went downstairs to get one. Quite inadvertently, I found the quietest path across the floorboards, down the back stairs and into the kitchen. There was one route, erratic but navigable, that would take you all the way without making the sort of racket that was sure to wake up at least half the house. I never managed to retain exact coordinates but would sometimes luck into it. That was what I was thinking about as I reached the kitchen and felt the stone slabs cold beneath my feet and knew that I had finished the trip as silently as I had ever done. Instinctively, the feeling brought me back to a summer in my childhood when I was nine and reading Fenimore Cooper for the first time, at my mother's suggestion. She sent me off for a summer at the Buzzards Bay house with a pair of buckskin moccasins, which I wore about every day and practiced running silently through the woods and onto the patio where my aunts took their evening cocktails. They always pretended to be shocked at my arrival, and my aunt Eileen would sometimes spill her drink and ask me to go inside and rummage another.

I was reliving some piece of that memory when I noticed, or came to understand, that I wasn't alone, that there were other figures nearby—outside, on the porch. At first, I thought perhaps someone had snuck out for a smoke or a late-night talk, but when I approached the window and got a better look, I realized what I was seeing. Three bodies. Two of them standing before another, who was sprawled out on the wicker daybed we kept outside with a thin, gingham cushion we were always meaning to replace. I had a glass in my hand. I had taken it from the drying rack intending to fill it but almost let it go. In fact, it slipped out of my grip but somehow I managed to catch it.

It was Valentina on the daybed. She was wearing a gray T-shirt I had bought her at the campus store some years before. It had cutouts in the shoulder. I don't know what moved me to buy it, but she pronounced it, immediately, ridiculous and wrong, a shirt fit for a fourteen-year-old girl and nobody else. But soon she began wearing it to bed, especially at the beach. Beneath it now, she wasn't wearing anything. In front of her, spreading her open, lowering down to begin the work, was Camille. She had her hair tied back. One hand was resting on Valentina's thigh. The other was reaching below, burrowing in, between the flesh and the gingham cushion.

Valentina's head was thrown back. Her throat looked so long at that angle.

And also beside them was Bruce. He was only watching at first. Then, he took a step closer, kneeled, and put his lips against the hand that was holding my wife's thigh.

Jesus Christ, I could see it all by the moonlight, clear as anything. It took what felt like a long time, long enough for my wife to be finished once at least, before I understood that it was a dream. I was asleep. Then came the relief and that sudden moment when you think, now that I know this, know that I'm dreaming, I can do anything. I can fly. I can shoot out of a cannon. But the knowledge doesn't last long enough to do much of anything with. By the time you perceive it, it's already dissolving, then it slips away.

Instead, I caught my breath. I wiped the sweat from my forehead. I was holding that glass, which in the dream I had almost dropped. I filled it up from the tap, looked once more on the porch to satisfy myself, then went back upstairs and saw my wife in bed with the sheets pulled over to her side, bunched up between her legs and wrapped around her neck, not like she was cold, but like she was trying to wring something out.

She always pulled at the sheets like that but was utterly convinced it was me who started, and she was only playing defense. She may have been right, too, though I didn't think so. It was one of those disputes that wasn't worth settling. Even if you filmed the whole night or asked an outside observer to make a ruling, neither of you would ever believe it. The sooner you recognize these things as quagmires, the better.

It was the séance, I thought. It was all just play, but still, it had disturbed me.

———⊙———

I slept in until some ridiculous hour. I couldn't remember the last time I slept so late. Valentina wasn't around, and I didn't make any special effort to find her. It was an ungenerous thing to have dreamed about your wife, and I didn't much want to see her just then and make the thing worse or pick a fight, so I decided instead to go for a swim.

It was a long swim, into the harbor and around the island that had once been connected by a rope-drawn ferry to the mainland. Nobody had lived on the island in over fifty years, but the osprey often circled it and made you think there was more going on out there than you understood. On the way back home, one of the birds locked on to me for a span of about a hundred yards, riding the winds overhead. I could see his shadow in front of me in the water, and it set a good pace and gave me something to swim toward on that empty stretch before Nanumett reared up and you could feel the inlet's pull.

By the time I got back, the afternoon was well along. I went look-ing for Camille in the garden room, wanting to ask her about the wallet—Bruce's wallet—but found Valentina there instead. She had her laptop open. Her notebooks were spread out around the desk. I could see she had been at it, working for hours. She coiled herself up when she worked like that, for a day without interruption. When she saw me through the windows, for a moment it seemed she didn't rec-ognize me. Then she waved me inside.

She said it was all right, she was just finishing, it was good of me to come and find her.

What was she doing in there? There were plenty of other rooms for her to work in.

"Let's go for a walk," she said. "Do you want to dry off first, or shower?"

I was still in my bathing suit, wet from the swim. I hadn't even bothered to towel off.

She decided we would go into the marsh, along a path that had been carved by the tide. I didn't much like being out there but hadn't a good reason why we should take a different route. It was a warm day and there was no coverage from the trees along the rim, but it wasn't the sun I was concerned about. The sun had been on my back all morning long and hadn't bothered me. In the flats, I noticed the fiddler crabs were out in great numbers. I would have thought the sun would drive them into their burrows, but maybe hunger brought them out in the daylight, where they were likely to get snatched by birds and bigger crabs. They always struck me as ravenous little creatures.

About two miles in, after we had circled back toward the house, keeping nearer to the water than before, we came across a small paddleboat. It was beached but in decent condition. It looked like somebody had rowed it in recently, then walked away. There were no footprints around, but there wouldn't be. The water would have erased them. It was also possible the boat had been swept over in the currents from Nanumett Beach.

"I'm going to sit," Valentina said.

I told her I would sit too. It was as good a time as any for a break.

There was something in the way she positioned herself on the rear bench of the boat that brought back to mind the dream: her, splayed on the daybed. She always knew when I was thinking mean things somehow. She said I might as well come out with it.

So I did, more or less. Told her as much as I was willing to get into just then.

"With both of them?" she asked.

"Yes."

"On the porch? En plein air? In flagrante?" She was teasing me. Feeling proud, maybe.

"I saw from the stairs," I said. "I could make it out clearly. There was no doubting it."

"No doubting that I was enjoying it?"

"Immensely."

She thought it over for a time. She had a way of making you feel less exposed, not because she was taking you so seriously but because she was listening to you at all. It was like we had gone on this walk precisely to find that boat, to have that talk.

"But you didn't want to join us?" she asked. Then, after a pause: "Be honest."

A hermit crab was walking along the bottom of the boat. He got close to Valentina's feet and pulled himself out of the shell to get a better look at her. A risky move, I thought.

"I had a dream too," she said. "It felt real. It was the night of the fireworks."

Did she want me to ask her to go on? People sometimes do when they're describing dreams. They want that piece of reassurance. But that wasn't it. She was just remembering. She never remembered her dreams, so it must have been odd for her.

"It was late in the dream," she said, "and I was out swimming. I saw you and Bruce on the beach fighting, and then a little while later he was swimming too. I told him to come along with me if he wanted. We could swim to one of the islands. He didn't want to, but I said something that I knew would make him go. I don't remember what it was."

"What do you mean we were fighting?"

"Rolling around. Punching. Kicking. All of it. You had something in your hand."

"But did you see us that night?"

"No, it wasn't like that. In the dream, it was just something that I knew."

"Then you told him to come swimming with you?"

She nodded. "He followed me. I swam out into the bay, into open water, nowhere near any of the islands. He couldn't tell where we were going. It was late. I just kept swimming and swimming. At some point he shouted to me, and I could hear he was almost out of breath. He could barely even call out. So I stopped and tread water until he caught up, but then when he got close again, I sort of pushed off backward. A few feet at a time. Have you ever seen a squid, the way it swims? It felt like that. I kept going backward, and he could barely move but he was trying to get to me. Maybe he would have tried to hang on to me, I don't know. Or he just wanted to feel something other than water. But I kept shooting myself backward, and eventually, he went under."

"He went under?"

"And didn't come back up. He drowned."

Her breathing had slowed, I noticed. She was so calm. It was just a dream, after all.

"I remember feeling relieved," she said. "I swam back to shore. Glad he was gone."

"But why would you be glad?"

"How would I know?"

"You're bothered by it?"

"It felt real, yes. So of course I was bothered."

"I mean, are you still?"

She thought it over before answering. "No, I wasn't, particularly. Until last night when they started calling out his name. Like he was dead. And throwing that wallet around. I kept wondering whether it was wet. That feel leather gets when it's been wet then dries. I was trying to see, and I almost asked her to hand it over so that I could touch it. It gets dry in a specific way, you can tell, and with seawater, there are sometimes salt streaks."

"It wasn't wet. She found it in a drawer. He didn't drown with it."

"But why hasn't he called to ask for it?"

"I don't know. He doesn't care. He got new cards. The cash, he forgot about, maybe."

"He doesn't forget anything."

"What does that mean?"

"Nothing. I only told you about it because you told me yours. Let's forget it."

But she didn't move. It felt like we were never going to leave that boat.

Or if we did, we were going to wait for the tide to come along and move it for us.

"I called his building," she said. "I kept trying his cell, but he wouldn't pick up, so I looked up his building, the management company, and they gave me a number to the doorman. I asked him when Bruce was by last, and the guy started speaking in Spanish. Just switched, out of nowhere. He's from Nicaragua. He told me Bruce hasn't been around in weeks, and the last time he saw him, he left some keys at the desk and said he was going to catch a boat. Then he offered to go upstairs to look inside the place."

"Inside Bruce's apartment?"

"I told him go ahead. Look. He said nobody's been there. Not even the cleaning lady."

She sounded angry now. Angry at who? For what? I felt quite lost with her.

"He didn't drown," I said.

"I know."

"He went on vacation. He went somewhere to write. He could be anywhere."

She looked around, not bothering to shield her eyes from the sun. "I know."

She locked in on an osprey, which was on its perch, watching us calmly. Normally they get agitated by a large body hanging around their territory, but this one seemed rather haughty, like it had been expecting us and had already agreed to extend its hospitality.

"I want to fool around," Valentina said and began taking off her clothes. "Come on."

She sounded somber about it, like there was no helping it, nothing to be done for it.

I lay my clothes beneath us, to help keep from getting splinters.

She was breathing into my ear. She did that sometimes, knowing how it affected me.

I came quickly. It felt like that was what she wanted. It didn't matter, really, how quick.

"They were dreams," she said, after we had dressed. "They mean nothing."

"I know."

"It's crazy to let them hang over us. To change our mood. To change anything."

She got up and stepped out of the boat. We didn't speak again until we reached the house, and then it was quite different, with everyone in the kitchen waiting for us, the kids included, wondering what to do about supper. They had laid all kinds of food out on the counter, like a puzzle that only had to be put together. It would all fit and a meal would come out of it. I didn't know what was making it feel that way, but nobody seemed especially hungry and the malaise that had

been hanging about the house earlier, when I had first woken up, was
lifted now. The air seemed cooler too.

—————————o—————————

In bed that night, I asked why she hadn't mentioned anything about
Rami and the girl.

"Which girl, Camille?"

"The other one. The girl in Budapest."

"Oh, the German girl."

Apparently, he had told her all about it the first thing on arriving.
I remembered that he had said, that night after he got in from the station, there was something he wanted to talk with me about. Maybe
that was it, but then he'd unloaded himself on Valentina instead.

"I'm sure that's not the first time he's gotten himself into that situation," she said.

"He said that it was."

"Really? That's surprising. I figured these things happen to men all
the time."

"It's never happened to me."

"Well, you don't attend a lot of trade negotiations."

That seemed to be the end of it. She was right, of course. I attended nothing, really.

When was the last time I'd gone anywhere without her or the
kids?

After a silence, during which I presumed she had fallen asleep, she said she hoped he was being more careful with Camille. She liked the girl. She liked them together, in fact.

Then she really was asleep. It wouldn't have done any good asking what she meant.

I got up and opened the drawer where I had stored away Bruce's wallet. He carried just three cards: his license, an American Express, and his health insurance card. The rest was the cash. It was $982 altogether. He had no souvenirs, no dry-cleaning chits, no subway card, no notes, and no receipts of any kind.

I thought maybe there would be a ferry ticket—a return—but there wasn't.

A short while later, I began to hear noises, thinking at first that they were only the house. But the house didn't make noises like that in summer. I went into the hallway to check what it was and realized it was coming from Rami's room. I went closer, without really interrogating the reasons why, until I realized what it was, then hurried back to my own bed as quietly as I could.

Through the open door, I had seen them: her on top, him beneath her, in the shadows.

So Valentina was right: They were sleeping together. It hadn't taken much time in the end. Mostly it was the bed making the noise but occasionally you would hear her breathing, too, very rapidly but measured, like she was trying to set them an even pace.

It was that metronomic quality that I found intriguing. Nobody had ever done that with me, and it seemed rather dogmatic and perhaps unpleasant, having those firm expectations hanging about as you tried simply to do your level best, but then I didn't think Rami would take it that way. He always thought the best of people and would have received the suggestion just as it was intended: as a way of bringing them together.

At least I thought he would. I really didn't know how he was with women. When I first met him at college, I thought him quite suave and worldly, then when I mentioned it to Maya and Shannon sometime later, they began to laugh. They didn't think that way of him at all. They thought he was sweet and often lovesick and whatever allure he had was built from those qualities. That had really left an impression with me, how we could have been seeing him from such different perspectives, forming entirely different conclusions about who he was and how he passed through the world. Yet we were such close friends, with an intimacy already well established. But then, intimacy doesn't guarantee agreement. Often, it's just the contrary, though it takes a long time to realize it.

19

Throughout the coming days, they began to appear more and more like a couple. There were no particular incidents or moments to relay, no hand-holding, no rolling around in the surf. It was more the consideration they began to show, and the feeling that they were looking for each other's consent, silent or otherwise, before undertaking things they had previously done alone. Rami, for example, would always check with her before leaving the house for his morning coffee. She didn't seem to want anything, but he would ask, and she would take time away from whatever she was working on to talk with him. It appeared to me to be those first moments of passion, when any separation begins to feel like a wound, when you notice that one is often bringing up the other in conversation just to hear the name spoken, or to speak it themselves, with some quiet knowledge of distinction, or even possession. I hadn't been around any new couples in quite a long time. In New Haven we probably came across them at parties or seminars, but I never knew what was going on, or who was screwing who, until Valentina told me.

One morning, Camille informed us that she and Rami were going to prepare dinner. They wanted to make something special. It sounded like a project she had been planning to get around to, like they'd always intended to do their fair share of cooking.

Rami went to do the shopping while Camille stayed behind, making a survey of the kitchen and what was around. They wanted to cook a Lebanese meal, but the store didn't have the right ingredients, so we were left instead with another eggplant dish, like the one Maya had put together weeks before, which had left us all hungry.

I was thinking that any night she would move into his room, or he would move into hers. The rooms were the same size, almost identical, though hers faced the marsh, while his looked out toward the beach and had a small ledge perched outside the window, where we had tried growing parsley one summer years before, with no luck.

As it turned out, we did have a room change. After dinner, the kids asked if they could move to the third floor. They said that it would be quiet there. The suggestion—that we, the adults, were thrashing about, making noise, drinking and chatting all hours—caught me off guard, and I agreed immediately, without asking anything more about it.

Valentina didn't object. Usually, she was left to make the decisions, and I supposed she was enjoying the momentary indifference and thinking that if anything much came of it—if they got scared up there alone, or if the lingering smell of wood-stain treatments bothered them—I would be the one to go deal with it since I had agreed in the first place.

Camille stopped me in the hall after and said how good it was.

"Twins always show that early independence," she said. "That resolve."

That night, as a light rain began then petered out, there was a proposal: We ought to play cards, a game of blush. I figured they were thinking we could be louder now because the kids had moved farther away. Someone got the tin of pennies out of the pantry, and we kept it going for an hour or more, working through three bottles of the green wine as we played. Toward the end of the hour, as the betting began to lag but nobody was quite ready to give it up entirely, Rami went on an incredible streak. He won twelve games in a row. I'd never seen anything like it, and yet nobody commented on the fact.

After we finished, I followed him outside. I asked if he might be going to walk the beach. In fact, we didn't get much beyond the yard. He had a joint with him, but there wasn't a light and he said that it wasn't worth going back in the house for the matches.

I asked what was wrong. It was clear he was out of sorts.

"Nothing," he said. "Nothing's wrong. I guess that must be what I'm waiting for."

I mentioned something about Camille and him and the dinner. It wasn't very subtle.

He didn't answer, so I asked him outright what was going on between them.

"I'm not exactly sure," he said. "It's all a little disorienting. To tell you the truth, I don't much like her. I mean, she's good-looking, although I can never be sure about that. Whether a person is actually attractive. You've always teased me about it, and you're right. My judgment, it's questionable, or worse even. But with her, I really don't know."

He sounded so confused.

"You don't know what?"

"Any of it. What she means. What we're doing."

"That could be a good thing. You're infatuated. Enjoy yourself."

He shook his head. "No, it's not that."

I remembered there was a matchbook on the windowsill of the shed. It was dry still.

"I'm feeling guilty about Bruce," he said. "We haven't cared. He went off. Fine, it's his decision. He's an adult. So are we. Except that the decent thing to do would be to feel sorry. What if it had been you who had gone off? Or me? We'd have sent out a search party. But the truth is, I want to forget about him. It's easier, pretending he never came at all."

"I do feel sorry."

"But you haven't called him."

"Valentina spoke to his doorman."

"To find out if he went home?"

I nodded. "We made an effort. Maybe not an enormous one, but . . ."

"I didn't make any effort," he said. "Not even a text. What does that say about me?"

"You get a few weeks off a year. You don't want to spend them feeling bad."

He breathed out slowly. "People don't just vanish. He should call, tell us where he is, even if he's angry. I would never do that, just go silent. You never would. It's not right. And then, I keep thinking, if something did happen to him, why aren't we looking? Why hasn't he turned up? It doesn't make sense to me. And here we are, on holiday."

"Enjoying ourselves."

"Having affairs. Flings. Like we're kids again."

He was digging the toe of his shoe into the dirt beneath us, like he was trying to turn something up. He was wearing a pair of expensive-looking pebbled loafers. I thought about a time once, years before, when I had complimented his sweater, and he made a gift of it to me.

It was too small, but I wore it often and was proud wearing it and never paid any attention to comments, like when Bruce asked if I had put it in the dryer.

"Anyway," he said. "I don't know what to make of her. She talks about her twins sometimes, then when I ask her about them, she laughs off the question, changes the subject. I thought at first, okay, she doesn't want to talk about her kids, so what? That's to be expected. At best, I'm a summer fling. Bruce was supposed to be one and he didn't stick around, so I'm taking his place. A warm body in her bed. Why should she tell me about her kids? But then, I don't know. She says things that make me begin to wonder."

"Whether she has any."

"Right."

"I've thought about that too."

"But it's crazy, don't you think? Why should we both wonder about that?"

I didn't know. I wasn't going to pretend. I had been assuming he understood the situation better than I did. He spoke French, for one thing. Maybe he overheard calls.

"No," he said. "She never calls anyone. I don't think I've even seen her use a phone."

He paused, like there was more.

"But then, I want her. I can't think straight around her. I forget everything."

That, I understood. Almost anyone could understand a thing like that.

"She's young," I said. "Maybe that's why she doesn't talk about her kids."

"Because she had them early?"

"She must have been a teenager."

We were both doing the math in our heads. Doing it blind, like the card game.

"Will you try to see her after?" I asked.

"After what?"

After his vacation, I had meant. After he went home. It seemed an obvious question.

Before I had a chance to explain, she came outside.

She sat down in a chair on the porch and faced us. She seemed quite content to watch.

She could hold herself very still. It was more than composure. Valentina had that too. In fact, there were many similarities between them, and I sometimes got the impression they were studying each other in an almost unconscious manner, without any particular purpose to their efforts, and in this way, were gradually growing more alike.

After a minute holding that position, she waved us over.

She was carrying a lighter and another joint. Where was everyone getting the stuff? Did we have a stash somewhere? Had we left it around, where the kids could discover it? We used to be so careful about what we left out but no longer were. That had changed.

She lit the joint and maybe it was the weed that prompted me: I asked about her kids.

"Clémence and Jean-Pierre," she said. "Very dull names but important for my family."

"Where are they this summer?"

"With their father. One can only presume they haven't run off. What else were you wondering about me? I was sure you were over there in the dark talking about me."

"We were talking about Bruce too," Rami said. "We were into all kinds of gossip."

She handed him her joint. He had put his away already, unlit.

"The thing that attracted me to Bruce," she said, "was his height. His posture."

Rami smiled, as she decided whether to go on.

"I like a tall man," she said. "A man who holds his shoulders back."

"That's natural," he said. "Even birds tend to their posture."

"But not everyone has the height to pull it off. Bruce, he had it."

"And is that all?"

It was simply banter, maybe. Or something else. As they were talking, I realized I was on the wicker daybed, and that they were positioned in almost precisely the places where I had seen Camille and Bruce that night, when I dreamed about the two of them with Valentina.

The thought of it excited me. It stirred something, imagining it again.

"I have to apologize to you," she said. Her attention had turned toward me.

"What for?"

"The séance. I meant for it to be fun. Calling the dead, all that. I didn't think how it might be different for you than for the others. Here, in this house. With your parents."

It felt like something Rami had prompted her to say. An apology owed, which had weighed on him. I told them it was nothing. I hadn't thought about my parents at all.

Camille put a hand on my arm, like I needed consoling, then took the joint back from Rami. "But how can that be?"

"Because I took it as fun, just as you meant it. I didn't think ghosts would arrive."

"You looked as though you were expecting someone," she said.

"Did I?"

"Yes. We all did. It's impossible, in that context, not to. No matter what you believe."

The statement hung around us for a while. Camille didn't pass the joint. She was holding it at her side, letting the light go out, thinking about something else, evidently.

"Your parents," she said, "they died in France, didn't they?"

I hadn't told her that. And yet there were any number of ways she might have learned of it. Valentina might have told her. Rami might have. She might have seen something lying around the house that I hadn't noticed in years, a document or an old photograph.

"They were visiting relatives?" she asked.

"Yes."

"Your mother was named Devereaux? She was French, then."

It disarmed me, hearing the words spoken, and I didn't feel like asking any more questions, or like talking at all, so I told them I had better get to bed before the weed hit.

"Good night, Jim," she said. "Sweet dreams."

Only she spoke in French. The phrases were familiar, somehow.

—————⊙—————

I was still lying in bed an hour later when the noise began. It sounded more like a wailing this time, but with the same rhythmic quality as the night before. I went into the hall thinking somebody else would be there, too, wondering what the matter was, or the kids would come downstairs, scared, but there was no sign of anyone. I was alone. The rest of the house, except for that one pulsing noise, seemed rather still and peaceful.

After a time—I don't know how long I was there—I looked down and was quite shocked to find I had something in my hands. It was the harpoon. But how had it gotten there? I must have been sleepwalking. I must have been asleep when I first went into the hall, and I had gone downstairs and taken it off the wall and brought it back up with me.

My mouth went dry, and the noise inside the bedroom ceased, suddenly. In the whole house, there wasn't a sound. I felt so utterly caught out and more ashamed than I had been since I was a child, and quickly I went downstairs, placed the harpoon on its mount, and hurried back to bed. Valentina hadn't moved in the time since I'd been gone.

20

We were all down at the beach, enjoying ourselves. Valentina and Shannon went out for a swim. Rami and Camille kept the kids busy most of the morning building a sandcastle. Une bastille, they were calling it. It had moats and turrets and a sort of drawbridge. For flags on top of the turrets, they had used leaves. There were always a few leaves that fell early near the beach and warned of the new season. Rami gathered a handful and spent a long time threading twigs and pine needles through them and positioning everything just so, to capture the sun. It looked rather glorious, once they were finished.

I must have been feeling grateful for the fineness of the day, because it caught me off guard later when Maya said something to question it. She was sitting in a beach chair, with a towel over her lap and a sweatshirt, in case she should need it, folded on top of a cooler between us. She took a sip of rum and said she wished she had somewhere to run off to but couldn't think of where to go. She had been thinking about it all morning.

"Like Bruce ran off," she said. "He must have left in the night, don't you think? Or better, first thing in the morning, before the sun. That's the time to run off. The predawn escape, I've always thought, is more romantic than stealing away, doing it at midnight."

I mentioned, as I had before, that her thoughts betrayed a certain restlessness.

She agreed. That was just it—she was feeling a tingle in her legs, trying to enjoy the sensation. "Shannon thinks I want to paint the girl. She told me she'd get the supplies."

"The girl?"

She nodded toward Camille, who was lying a few yards away next to the bastille.

The kids had gone off with a few of the neighbors to look for crabs on the jetties. Maybe they were thinking about putting the crabs in the castle, if they caught any. We had done that once, and they hadn't gone anywhere but sort of scuttled around making themselves at home, until finally the tide came in, and the bay swallowed them back up.

"Do you want to paint her?" I asked.

She shook her head. "I wouldn't mind sitting in a room with her for a few hours, let's see what happens. Nothing, maybe, but I would get to imagine all kinds of depravities, you know? That's the best part sometimes, just sitting in a room with someone whose portrait you're going to paint, and you get to be still and silent and think horrible things. They don't know. They can't. They assume you're just working out the light."

"It sounds uncomfortable to me."

"You haven't thought about it?"

"Painting her?"

"What you'd do to her."

I paused before answering, and in the pause, she seemed to believe, was my answer.

"Shannon thinks about it," she said. "The pregnancy gets her riled up, I noticed. She tugs at the sheets at night. She got this pillow that's about five feet long and sort of winding, like a snake, so that's what I call it. The snake. The serpent. Python. It's supposed to help her sleep on her side during the last months, but it goes between her legs, and God help me, Jim, I see her rubbing against the thing sometimes. She doesn't know what she's doing. She's asleep. I don't have the heart to tell her, come morning. She found it online somewhere. It's supposed to be this wonderful thing to have, for side sleeping, through the final trimester. Women swear by these pillows."

At that last statement, she raised her glass, as though it were a toast.

I was searching for something reassuring to say, when she cut me off and asked whether she ever told me about Professor Prozorova and the letters she wrote. It was an abrupt question, seemingly unrelated, but I could see she was in a mood to talk.

Professor Prozorova was a woman who taught Russian civilization courses that were another part of the core requirement when we were at school. There were lots of vestiges of the Cold War still hanging around. They were training us all to be a very particular kind of diplomat, in a very particular world, which already no longer existed.

No, I said, she had never told me about any letters.

She laughed, like it was funny. "She wrote me a letter, sometime toward the end of senior year. She said that she felt our souls had spoken to one another, that I was a beautiful person. She was going to move to Prague to be with her husband. Do you remember the husband? He was somebody big in the Orthodox Church, a clergyman."

I did remember. He would come to campus dressed in black vestments.

She took another sip of the rum and went on. "He was being sent to Prague and she was going to join him for a year at least. She proposed that I go too. To live with them."

"To live with them?"

"She said she had cleared it all with him. He was on board, I guess. This was in the letter. It was this really intricately written letter. I can still picture it so clearly. This tiny little script, and all the paragraphs ending and beginning at different points, different margins. In this brown ink. She wanted me to go to Prague, to be their lover for a year."

Their lover. What a thing to propose. And she had never told me.

"That's kind of flattering," I said, "in a lunatic way."

She nodded. That was what she thought as well, exactly so: flattering and lunatic.

She was glad I thought so. She had always wondered what I would make of it.

"I didn't tell anybody about this," she said. "I walked around with this love letter for a week. Then one day I went by your place, early. I was up early in those days, maybe bothered about this letter I was carrying around. I let myself into your house and Bruce was there at the kitchen table with a coffee, one of those big breakfasts he used to cook. Right away, I noticed something strange. He had this paper in front of him at the table."

"A letter?"

"He had gotten one too. It wasn't exactly the same, but the gist of it was: he was beautiful, she thought he'd benefit from a year of being her and her husband's lover."

"In Prague."

"Right, in Prague. Isn't that crazy?"

I was trying to picture Professor Prozorova: a small woman, sol-idly built, with a great mass of black hair, streaked with white. It went all the way down her back. She sometimes used to brush it while she delivered her lectures. She had seemed to me to be a woman well into her fifties, though in retrospect I wasn't sure.

She could have been younger than that. Maybe the same age we were now.

She never referred to any notes when she lectured. She would just brush her hair, or sometimes walk around the classroom and stop in an unexpected place—a corner or by the door. She had never struck me as very passionate, though what did I know about it?

"After that," Maya said, "we asked you all questions about her. Do you remember it? We would find ways of mentioning her in conversa-tion. Or her husband. The two of them. We were trying to figure out who else got the letters. We decided it was only us."

"I never got one. I'd remember that. I've never been to Prague."

"I never wanted to go. Fuck Prague. Bruce did, though."

"He wanted to go with them?"

"Maybe. I think he liked that they had picked him out to ask. Or the two of us, as it turned out. I kept feeling like he was waiting for me to suggest we go ahead, try it out. That we move to Prague, with these two batty old sexpot Russians. And live off what?"

"They would have supported you. It's implicit, in the letter, the in-vitation."

"No, I don't think so. He thought he could get a fellowship. He kept saying that."

It was true. I remembered, toward the end of school, Bruce was always talking about fellowships. He seemed to believe they were ev-erywhere, all around, there for the taking, and they were the key to whatever would come next. But as far as I knew, he never applied for anything. He may well have, but he had never mentioned them to me.

But then, he hadn't mentioned the letter either.

Neither of them had mentioned it, in all those years. It was their peculiar secret.

"Don't run off," I said. "Not to Prague or anywhere. Valentina would kill me."

"I don't think she'd mind so much."

"She wants me to persuade you and Shannon to stay here."

"We are here."

"For longer, I mean. I don't know why, but it's been on her mind. She keeps saying I should tell you that the sea air is good for a newborn. It helps clear their congestion."

"Is that true?"

I figured it was. I had a vague memory of the twins, always clogged up at the start.

"I don't want to paint anyone," she said, "and I can't think of where to run off to. If I didn't go to Prague at twenty-one with the Russians, I must be a hopeless case. It's all this sitting around, taking in the air. It's cleaned me right out of ideas. I'm enjoying myself. But Shannon has so much energy. She doesn't know what to do with it all, so she goes swimming and tells me to paint young things lying around, driving her wild."

"Valentina had that: that excess. I thought pregnancy was supposed to be depleting."

"Not for them. For me, it would have been. I get tired just thinking about it."

Camille came over just then and dropped down between us. Her legs were caked with sand, and there were streaks on her arms too.

She must have been wet when she lay down. I looked over and saw that Rami had fallen asleep there, beside the sandcastle.

She shielded her eyes against the sun and looked at Maya, then at me, smiling.

"I've been wondering what the two of you are talking about so intently," she said. "I couldn't think of any pretense for intruding and finding out, so I've simply come."

"We were talking about you," Maya said.

Her tone wasn't flirtatious. It was matter of fact. I was struck by it. It reminded me of the way, the night before, Rami had launched into a new conversation with her and had seemed, in doing so, to be an entirely different person than the one I had been speaking with up until that point. It was unnerving, watching a person, a friend, change like that.

Camille didn't respond. She was brushing sand from the underside of her arms.

"I'm going to paint you," Maya said. "But not just yet. Some other time."

Camille leaned back. Not a pose, but not an entirely natural movement either. She was showing us her neck, it seemed. Turning this way and that in the sun to let us get a look.

"You should paint the house," Camille said. "Don't spend your time on people. Certainly not on people like me. If I had any talent at all, I would paint this house."

Maya looked at her and at the house. "You would?"

"Yes, I think it's beautiful. If I had any talent, I'd try."

It was strange, because I'd had much the same thought not so long before, when Shannon had first told me that Maya wasn't going to work or think or do anything while they were visiting. I had been disappointed, hearing that, because already it had occurred to me I might empty out the boat shed for Maya to use. That shed had a good steel sink where she could wash her brushes and two windows, one facing the water and the other with a pleasant angle on the house. She would get a cross-breeze in there and—this was the thing—I thought maybe she would be moved to paint her surroundings. She might stay out there awhile and want to paint the house, or perhaps the beach, that very stretch of beach where we were now sitting, which in fact was Maya's property as much as it was mine. That was arranged long ago. There was no undoing it. It was a stupid thought, though. I knew she had no interest in landscapes.

"I think," Camille said, beginning slowly, as though she were choosing her words carefully, "that perhaps there's something a bit awkward hanging between you just now. All of you. Some of you, in any case. Would you like to know what I think it is?"

Her eyes had narrowed. It may have only been the sun, but it made me think of what Maya had said before, about her being a provocation, and what she would think about if you put them together alone in a room for a few hours with some paints and a canvas.

"How did you find your donor?" she asked.

Maya's face turned slightly. Before, she had been smiling, enjoying the girl's bravado.

"Our donor?"

"For the baby. You never asked your friends, did you? You used a service."

"No," Maya said. "We didn't ask them."

"But why not? Did it ever occur to you? Only Jim has children, a family of his own. Perhaps Rami or even Bruce would have liked to be asked. Would have been honored."

"Our goal wasn't to honor anyone. It was to have a baby."

"Was it you or Shannon who first had the idea? About the baby, I mean?"

I couldn't tell whether Maya was warming to the subject or trying to.

"Her idea first. But when she said it, it felt like something I had been thinking about."

Camille smiled. "Isn't it wonderful when that happens with an idea?" Then she looked again at Rami. He seemed in no danger of waking anytime soon. "But perhaps you wanted a particular baby, and it didn't make sense for the donation to come from them."

"Yes, that was it. We wanted a particular baby."

Just then, Valentina and Shannon appeared, coming to dry land. They had been out for some time, but neither of them seemed in the least to be struggling over the final yards.

Camille said she was going up to the house. If Rami woke up, could we tell him?

Maya turned in her chair to watch her walk away.

"She's got some fucking nerve."

Yes, I agreed. She had. That was one thing you could call it.

Maya held up her glass and moved around the ice. "The strange thing is, I did wonder about that. I wondered if any of you were offended at not being asked. Shannon said not to be stupid. Of course you weren't. Why would we ask you? Why put that responsibility between us? Friends don't do that sort of thing. Were you?"

"Offended?"

"Thinking we might have asked you."

"Never."

"What about him?"

She was looking over to where Rami carried on sleeping. It was lucky he never burned.

"Not that he ever told me."

"What would you have done, if we had asked?"

It had never occurred to me before. I had to think about it for a while.

"I would have said yes. Of course I would have."

"And would it have been strange for Valentina?"

"I think she'd have been glad."

That made Maya laugh. It came out quickly, through her nose, at first.

"I think you're underestimating the complications," she said. "That's kind."

She sounded very sure of herself, and I felt stupid for having answered that way.

Then, as Valentina and Shannon got closer, Maya said, her voice lower, conspiratorial, "Don't tell Shannon any of that stuff about Prague, all right? I never mentioned it to her. She'd tease me about it. That's just the kind of thing she gets her hooks in and never lets go of."

"All right, I won't."

"Don't tell her about that donor stuff either. Shit, just assume I'm drunk, okay? You wouldn't repeat anything said to you by a drunk woman. I know you wouldn't, Jim. You're too fucking decent for that. If manners were genetic, we would have asked you."

Now I was the one laughing. I had always thought of manners as being one of Rami's defining characteristics, in fact. His parents were very sophisticated, bighearted people.

21

During the next few days, I noticed Rami growing increasingly preoccupied and wondered whether he was falling in love. He had sounded so ambivalent about whatever was going on between him and Camille, I figured there was at least the possibility it had become something serious or was headed that way. Maybe she had put that very question to him. She didn't seem to me to have much delicacy, so the confrontation, if there had been one, might have been rather blunt. In any case, I knew they were enjoying themselves at night. Then one afternoon he proposed we take a walk on the beach. I guessed that, in the course of it, he was going to try explaining to me what was going on, ask for my advice, or perhaps he wanted company while he brooded. We made it nearly as far as the public boat launch before finally getting into it.

"She's gone," he said. "She left last night. I thought I ought to tell you. To be honest, I wasn't sure she really had, but her things were packed and gone from her room. She had left some clothes in my dresser, and those were gone too. It's the strangest thing. I could understand it if we had fought. Or if she had said anything at all about wanting to leave, or needing to. Like she had to get back to her kids.

But she didn't give any indication. Who does that? I know I shouldn't take it personally, but fuck it, I have to."

It took me a moment, and a few questions, to catch up with him. He still had that preoccupied air, and it felt like talking to someone who had already asked themselves all the questions you could possibly ask and had turned up insufficient or inadequate answers. Camille had left the house, apparently. He really couldn't understand. She managed it very quietly, in the night. A car came for her, he presumed.

We went over to the pier and had lunch at the restaurant on the deck of the old taffy shop and talked it over some more. I was trying to figure out whether he wanted to be consoled or if it was only a story, a somewhat troubling one, whose shape he was still working out. He said that it was true what he had told me before, they hadn't fought, not exactly, but there had been a kind of disagreement between them, yet it had seemed to him such a meaningless one, and he couldn't believe it had anything to do with motivating her to take off. She had asked him about his first time with a woman. He hadn't wanted to talk about it. He tried making a joke out of it, something about being chivalrous, about how she wouldn't like to think he was talking about her with other people, other women down the line, and she had said that was stupid, of course he would talk about her with other people. Why should he want to keep her such a secret?

"We were twisting one another's words," he said. "It felt like we were both being careful, speaking slowly, knowing that the other was listening and might decide to pounce. But pounce isn't the right word. Because it really wasn't a fight. Just sparring."

"It sounds ordinary," I said. "Everybody spars like that."

"You and Valentina do?"

"And worse. It sneaks up on you. Starts out fun, then takes a turn."

"But about what?"

"It doesn't matter. That's the point. It's what you're describing. A feeling that she's listening too closely. Not for the meaning of the words but how she can use them. It's unnerving. I don't know what I'm saying half the time—why should she use that against me? Then I do the same to her. We've learned to be more careful, I suppose."

He was trying to take what I had to say to heart, but you could tell it confounded him.

"I'm not used to arguing," he said. "Not so intimately."

"Call her. Find out what happened."

He shook his head. Apparently, it was out of the question.

When we got back to the house, he told the others a condensed version of the same story he had told me: that Camille had left in the night, that he didn't know why or whether she was coming back, but he suspected not. Already the story sounded more discernible, like there was a heavy fatefulness to their relationship from the beginning.

"What are you talking about?" Shannon said. "She was just here. We saw her."

Rami looked quite taken aback. "You saw her?"

"I spoke with her in the kitchen. She hasn't gone anywhere. You're so dramatic."

We went to her room, all of us together. We must have looked quite odd, as a pack.

The room was empty, as Rami had said it would be. Her things were gone.

We went downstairs and checked the garden room, which she had been using as an office. It had been cleared out too. The only thing there was Bruce's charger, which I had left plugged into the wall since he had gone. Shannon said it didn't make any sense.

"Maybe she forgot something," Rami said. "She came back for it and told the car to wait for her. She popped inside to get the one thing. Probably she didn't want you to worry."

Shannon looked at him sideways. "But why would I worry?"

"I don't know," he said. "Maybe she's a sociopath. I really don't know."

Valentina put an arm around him and told him not to worry, she would find him a new girl. There was plenty of summer left. She would dig up another French girl, if he liked.

—— ◇ ——

That night after dinner I think we were all waiting around for some sign of her return. We stayed up later than had been our habit recently, and it felt, to me anyway, like the darkness on the marsh was always on the cusp of being broken by a flash of headlights. Nobody came. There were no messages. Rami kept checking his phone, though eventually he admitted he didn't think she would text. Texting wasn't like her.

At one point in the evening, the sky took on a red hue, and I remembered it was Illumination Night. It was just another summer tradition now, like any other, like the Fourth of July, except the flares they lit, all along the harbor beach, would make less noise than the fireworks did, and the crowd that turned out for the lighting ceremony was mainly composed of the old families, the ones who stayed year-round.

We'd been, but not lately. I hadn't even known it was happening until I saw the light. They kept the date a secret. There were no fliers, no ads as there were on the Fourth, when they raised money by putting a cartoon thermometer in the local paper. Every week the temperature rose slightly, until finally they had enough money for fireworks.

The flares didn't seem to require fundraising. One of the families owned them, likely.

Valentina shook her head. "I don't like them in groups."

"Who?" Shannon asked. "The Patuxens? Is that what they're called?"

Yes, I told her. That was what they were called. Patuxens.

Valentina went on. "There's something unnatural about them when they get together. Feels like they've got cousins or sisters or aunts or wives locked up at home. That's what all the attics and basements are for. And they're looking us over. Making a decision. Like it's a town meeting. That's exactly how they look, I bet, at the meetings."

"Deciding on what?"

"Whether we're worth marrying, locking up. Worth all that trouble. The attic space."

Shannon reached over and took her hand. "Oh, sweetie. I'm sorry to break it to you."

Valentina laughed. I thought at first it was a private joke, something already shared.

"I know," she said. "They already got me. Married, locked up, all of it."

It had never occurred to me that she thought of me as one of them.

I was about to mention that she was the one who wanted me to persuade Maya and Shannon to stay on, to spend the fall at the house, and possibly the winter too: to keep the baby on the coast, where the salt air would clean out its sinuses. But it felt like too stinging a comment just then. They were all talking lightly, treating the subject like it was nothing, which I understood was the better course, rather than starting a squabble.

What was there to object to, anyway? She was right about Illumination Night. The hundred who showed up always stood very close together, though there was a great swath of beach there in the inner harbor, near the pier, where they started lighting the torches. The night they chose for the lighting was based on something: the moon, for all I knew. It was an odd thing to carry on. I was grateful the kids never asked about going.

Now I knew Valentina wanted no part of it either.

Still, I found it strange that we had never discussed it, exactly. It seemed she had very set notions about what it was, and I tried remembering if there was ever a summer when she went off to see it for herself. She must have, from the way she described it all.

———————◦———————

In the morning, when I got downstairs, Rami asked again if we could talk. I thought he meant another beach walk, and I told him I had promised the kids we would go for an early swim. He didn't seem to hear me. His attention was on something outside, in the marsh. It looked like he'd seen something out there and was waiting for a re-appearance.

"Last night," he said, "I dreamed I had killed her out there."

I stepped in closer, as though I hadn't heard him clearly.

"We were arguing about something in bed. I was asking her not to be so loud, not to shout, because she'd wake the kids. It wasn't anyone but the kids I was thinking about, and for some reason it made her furious, when I mentioned it. Because she has kids of her own, was my sense. She ought to know better than me what would wake them up."

He had the coffee made already. He poured me a cup, though I hadn't asked for it.

"I'm sorry," he said, "to bore you with this."

"I'm not bored. Everyone's been telling their dreams lately."

He nodded, like that was what he had expected I would say, and he appreciated it.

"We went outside to fight louder," he said. "Outside, she could shout as loud as she pleased. That was what she kept saying, and we were walking farther into the marsh, along one of the paths, because she said she wanted us to be alone, finally, so that she could shout anything she liked. I was trying to stop her. To say we'd gone far enough. But she didn't think so. She really wanted to shout fucking loud, so we kept going. Until we found a rowboat in the mud. She liked the look of it and said she might do some good shouting inside of that boat. She was screaming. I couldn't get her to stop."

He paused, and I mentioned that in fact there was a rowboat in the marsh, stranded.

"Is there? I must have seen it. I must have walked by it without re-alizing. In the dream, I had never seen it before, but she was scream-ing in there and wouldn't stop, and I kept thinking the kids would hear. Even from all the way out there. So I picked up an oar and whacked her across the face. Caved in her skull. Then did it again and came back home and woke you up and asked you a lot of questions. It was fucking awful, all of it."

"Questions about what?"

"About diplomatic immunity. Whether it worked for more than parking tickets. If I needed to declare it at the airport or could just get out and call the police about it later."

I put my hand on his shoulder. He was warm. You could feel the heat rising off him.

"It was just a dream," I said. "It's been going around, that sort of thing."

"I know. It'll just take me a few minutes to get rid of it, I think. I'll go for a swim."

"Come with me and the kids."

"No, I think I better go alone."

He turned to go upstairs, then stopped and looked back.

"I probably should have been asking Valentina," he said.

"Asking her what?"

"The questions. About diplomatic immunity. Do you know anything about it?"

"Nothing at all."

He nodded again, like that was precisely the confirmation he needed. I turned back toward the window, looking out at the marsh, and watched for a while. At that hour, with the sun still coming up, it appears that the horizon is moving, but it's only a trick.

n the afternoon I shuffled around streets in the village center, inventing errands and thinking in the back of my mind I might see her coming out of a coffee shop or the grocery store and she would explain what happened. A piece of me was outraged, I suppose. It wasn't the first time our hospitality had been used up and then thrown out.

I went to the Spiritualist camp and walked roughly the same path she and I had made through the clearing some weeks before, looking over the buildings, but I was alone now and didn't like the feeling of it. I soon went back to the center by High Street.

A brief shower rushed in off the water and sent everyone scurrying about. It reminded me of the days I had come to inspect the house after my aunts had died. I had been living in New York for several years at that point, and the town felt so small to me, except when it rained, then it seemed that there was a great mass of people hiding around in nooks and dugouts, waiting to scurry from one shelter to the next the moment the rain arrived. It was a place that enjoyed the damp, or at the very least thrived in it, knowing all the ways the water could be gathered and used.

I was near the library as the rain picked up and thought it was as good a spot as any to wait things out. The lights were dim. For a moment I wasn't sure it was open. It was often closed unexpectedly. Sometimes it was simply the lunch hour, and you would have to wait for the librarians to return. It was a small operation, though somehow the administrators managed to find the budget for archivists and air conditioners running night and day all summer. They probably used up half their budget on cool air.

In the back room, alone at a desk, working under lamplight, was Miss Huxley. I must have at least considered the possibility of discovering her there. She glanced up from some papers and saw me looking rather damp and as though I had thrown on my sandals at the very last moment before coming inside. She didn't seem to relish the prospect of addressing me, or of being addressed, and yet she seemed also to expect me.

"It'll blow over in twenty minutes," she said, meaning the rain, I presumed.

"I'm glad I ran into you, anyway."

She nodded, without committing herself. She was wearing a sweater this time. The chore coat she'd worn to the house was hanging on a peg on the wall, just behind her.

I said that I was wondering if she had heard from Camille. It seemed to take her a moment to place the name. There was a chair beside her, and I sat down in it. It felt like we were the only two people in the library, though it was entirely possible there was somebody in a back room, or perhaps others in the stacks who'd come in from the rain.

"That night," she said, "was my one and only experience with that woman."

"It was? I thought she had been in touch with you before."

She shook her head. "It ended none too soon. I don't mean to be rude, having come into your home, accepting that invitation, but I'll tell you, since I'm a woman who believes plain speaking is always a better course and more prudent: I won't be going back soon."

It was such a roundabout yet forthright statement, I didn't know what to say next.

"Did something happen?"

She looked at me carefully. It was the first time she had really studied me since I approached. She had crow's lines all around her face, especially around the eyes, and together they seemed to concentrate all the wisdom and skepticism implied by the rest of her appearance. It was strange the woman should present such an overwhelming impression of doubt, given her area of expertise. It bestowed a certain confidence in her, somehow.

"Look," she said, "if there's something you'd like to ask me, ask it. I don't believe in subtlety. Subtlety is prevarication in sheep's clothing. So, young man, let's have a frank conversation, or let's be quiet through the rain. Choice is yours, but I'll tell you, I'd just as soon go back to my papers."

I really didn't feel I had anything to ask, or rather, anything more than I had already asked her, about Camille being in contact, yet she seemed so sure of herself and of me.

"Did you . . . sense something when you were in our home?"

She raised a single gray eyebrow. "Of course I sensed it. Didn't you?"

"I don't think so."

"But you're asking now about the woman."

"Because she left."

"She's gone? When did she leave?"

"She had an argument with one of my friends. And the next morning, she was gone. Her room was cleared out. She must have taken a taxi or walked into town. But there was no sign of her. I thought maybe someone in town gave her a ride or noticed her around, but nobody has. It's odd, a person walking off like that. No word as to why."

The woman's eyes seemed to be narrowing all the time I was talking. "She didn't go anywhere. That's your first mistake, believing that horseshit. Telling yourself all that."

"She's gone. We checked her room. She packed up and left."

She sighed. "Your house was a place I had been wanting to visit. I should have told you that before, but I waited. Better to be invited, with a house like that, was my thinking. And yet, when I got there, I felt unwelcome. Do you know what I mean when I say that word? *Unwelcome.* I don't believe you do. The house is yours. Before that, it was in your blood. So how could you know what it means to step foot inside and feel that? You couldn't, really. The matter was, and I've come to believe this wholeheartedly, on reflection, the invitation came from that woman. Not from you. Not in the family line."

"I don't understand what that means."

"You've got an undesirable presence. An interference. I've come across all sorts of spirits in my time, felt all manner of interferences, forces that want to muck up channels, cause confusion. They have designs of their own. We don't know what they are at first."

"But . . . she's not a spirit. That's not what we're talking about."

"What do you know about it? You came here asking, so I'm telling you."

She was looking at me with great force of conviction. But I sensed, also, there was another part of her that truly didn't care what I thought or what I understood from her.

"That house," she said, "is troubled. You better figure what it wants."

"It's not troubled," I said. Then added, rather half-heartedly, "That's absurd."

"You've been getting messages, haven't you? You and everyone who lives there. You'll go on getting messages, communications, until you start listening to what it wants. That's been the way of it, for me. But I don't say I'm any expert in satisfying the things."

"I thought that's exactly what you were."

She shook her head forcefully. "I can hear them. Talk to them sometimes. That's all. Think talking to them means I know what to do, how to give them what they want?"

She began laughing, like it was the funniest thing she had heard in quite some time.

When she was done, we sat in silence and listened as the rain gathered strength.

At one point, Miss Huxley made an effort to return to her papers. I felt like I had already gone. I then asked another question that was on my mind, without warning.

I asked whether she knew my parents when they were alive. If she had ever met them.

"Yes," she said, slowly, without showing any surprise at the turn we had taken. "Your mother wanted to see the letters around the house's construction. We spent an afternoon going over everything there was. Your father waited outside, I remember."

"Why did she want to see the letters?"

"She didn't say. I liked her, I'll tell you that. Beautiful woman. Refined, in the classic sense. It was goddamn awful what happened to her. To both of them. I was sorry for it."

"Why did my father wait outside?"

"He wasn't wearing shoes. At that time, things were more strict. So he waited."

I thought carefully over my next question before asking it, deciding if I wanted to.

"And have you contacted them since?"

She smiled. "Since they passed over? I haven't. Have you?"

The rain was giving up now, and she stood from her chair and walked over to the window. There was a gutter overhead, which was still pouring down a steady stream.

She looked at it quite resentfully. Her breath was fogging the glass.

"I don't like the rain," she said. "People expect me to. They think I must go in for all that melancholy nonsense. I'll tell you what I like: sunshine. Enough to burn the skin right off your back if you're dumb enough. I want to wake up every day, find it's so goddamn sunny I can hardly walk straight. But I live here. Who the hell knows why?"

It felt like she was dismissing me. Like I had been summoned. And now expelled.

23

oming out of the library, I was still under the influence of the rather confounding things Miss Huxley had suggested, and I was looking forward to the walk back to the house and thinking I might extend it some ways, going along the eastern bank of the salt pond, where the trail veered off and took a detour of a half mile or so into the woods. Because of all the water in town, when you were on foot you could always count on there being another route. Each one was slightly more circuitous than the last.

While I was passing the final storefront that made up the town center—a real estate office—I noticed someone across the way, heading in the opposite direction. I noticed her first, it seemed to me, by her shadow. There are a hundred different markers by which we recognize those closest to us. Who's to say which one is the clincher in a given encounter, especially one like that, when I wasn't expecting to see anybody I knew, and it was only by sheer chance, or something even more erratic than chance, that I should see my own wife walking by, wearing a sweater tied around her waist, in a style I had never seen her wearing a sweater before. Her jeans were torn at the knees. Above that she was wearing a tank top, and I was struck by what a dark, rich color her shoulders had turned. She was looking in a storefront across from the one I had just passed. It was another real estate office. It was a wonder the two of them could survive.

Without giving the matter much thought, I stepped out of sight and waited as she continued in the direction she was headed, toward the center. I turned back that way myself, and it felt quite ordinary at first, like I only meant to surprise her. Any moment, I would run from behind and put a hand around her waist or maybe slide it into her back pocket. She had done that to me before and I remembered enjoying the sensation, the jolt of it, the fear. But I kept hanging back and only watched her instead. She didn't go inside anywhere. She wasn't carrying a shopping bag or anything else. She was unencumbered and seemed merely to be out walking for the sake of it, for the pleasure.

When she went onto the pier, I kept back and watched from across the street and realized after a few minutes that I was in precisely the same spot where Rami and I had sat in the Jeep and waited for the ferry to come and deposit Bruce, that first day, when he arrived. She was sitting on a bench by the ferry landing. The boat wasn't due in for several hours, but it looked like she was waiting for something, or somebody, out there.

Then, after a time, she simply walked away. If she was disappointed in some manner, it didn't show, not from that distance. I was thinking it was time to quit whatever I was doing and go talk to her, say how funny, how strange it was to run into her like this. I didn't, and in that moment of indecision she went into McGinty's, the Irish pub across from the pier. She appeared a moment later in the bay window with a beer in front of her. The beer was served in a tall, narrow glass. What was she doing drinking beer? Had she ever ordered one with me? I didn't think she had in all the time I'd known her.

I knew I should leave her be or go talk to her, but I didn't do either. I just stood there and watched. That was what I was doing sometime later when I heard my name called.

My first thought, on hearing it, was that I'd been caught. But it turned out to be only Tom Shaw waving me down from half a block off, hurrying over in my direction, looking like we had planned to meet up in precisely this fashion, there on the sidewalk.

I asked how he was, and he told me. He was one of those people who believe others really wish to know. They go through life never interrogating any of the premises that drive them. He told me about a cold he had been fighting, which he said had begun in his knees and had finally returned there, so he felt like he was walking around bow-legged. Did I know the sort of cold he meant? I was keeping an eye on Valentina in the bar window as we spoke. She hadn't moved since sitting down. Tom didn't seem to notice. He asked whether I'd heard the latest. He figured I must have heard all about it.

"About what?" I asked.

"The squatters," he said. "Those kids, they nabbed 'em again. You believe it?"

He then told me the story, which somehow seemed to mirror the story of his summer cold in its basic, circular structure. The kids they had found squatting in the Canham house had been let out after a week, Tom said, on some sort of technicality, then they had gone right back to it, laying down camp inside another empty house, this time in the Bellingham place on the Neck, doing it up the same way as before, gathering a big load of mattresses and dropping them down in the living room so they could all be together. "You imagine that? Like they were trying to make a point out of it. Taking a stand, going right back to what they were doing, like there's nothing anybody can say."

He seemed quite put out by the situation.

I didn't think he was related to the Canhams or Bellinghams, though he may have been.

"What we ought to do," he said, "is go by the jail, a group of us, and talk to them."

He said the word *talk* pointedly, so that you would know what he really meant.

"Why would we do that, Tom?"

"Why not? Somebody's gotta teach those kids the rules of civilization."

The rules of civilization. It was such a preposterous, eloquent phrase, I laughed.

He didn't think it was funny. "Well, someone should. You may not care much about keeping your house in order, but I do. There are more like me than aren't, I'll bet you."

"I'm sure you're right."

"What's that supposed to mean?"

His tone was turning angry, the less sure he got of himself.

"Nothing, Tom. I've gotta go, that's all."

"You were standing here ten minutes. I saw you before I went into the post office."

"So what?"

"So now you're in some big rush, huh? The hell with you."

But he didn't move, and neither did I. We were standing rather close, in fact.

"Those kids were in your house too," he said. "But it's nothing to you. Big house, must be nice. Place so big you don't care who the hell goes inside, who screws around in it. It's the kind like you who gives them ideas. Makes 'em think there's no consequences."

"Nobody was squatting in my house, Tom."

"The hell they weren't. I talked to George. I know how you found the place."

"What does it matter to you how I found my house?"

He stepped back finally and shook his head, disgusted. He'd been drinking, I gathered.

"I want to know," I said. "What's it to you, Tom? It's not your house."

"You think you're the fucking lord of the manor, don't ya?"

I realized—a beat late—he was stepping back in order to take a swing at me. It was an awkward movement, and he didn't seem too sure of it himself, or maybe he lost confidence halfway through. The result was a rather clumsy coming together. His arm wrapped my neck, our chests bumped, and his footing became unsteady. I held him upright, locking him in, then he pushed me back and managed in doing so to fully fall this time. It was the curb behind him that did him in. From one knee, he looked disgustedly at the curb, then at me. He soon got himself upright again and dusted off.

Then, as if nothing had happened, he spoke in a calm and measured voice. "I just thought you should know what's going on. If it doesn't bother you, that's your business. But a man ought to keep his neighbors informed. That's what it's all about."

He seemed pleased with this statement of principle and carried himself off under its steam, leaving me alone again. I turned back to the bar and saw that Valentina was gone.

I thought maybe she was only getting herself another tall beer to sit with for a while, but when I went inside to see, the place was empty, except for two old men hovering over a game of backgammon and the bartender, who was reading a book in the corner.

24

That night, after dinner, Valentina mentioned she had to go away for a few days, maybe a week. There was a faculty dispute erupting in New Haven, and people were being called in. It sounded nasty, whatever was unfolding, but I noticed that she didn't seem reluctant to get in the middle of it. She was probably looking forward to some time to herself, even if it would be punctuated by a lot of meetings and memos and straw votes.

"You'll enjoy some time without me," she said. "You'll have more fun than you've had all summer. Just make sure the kids eat something other than cereal. And that Rami doesn't wallow. Tell him I said it's not worth wallowing over, any of it. I told him, but he'll take it to heart if he knows we've been talking about him, too, behind his back."

While she was packing her suitcase, I tried describing to her some portion of the afternoon's events. I told her, anyway, about the library, and what Miss Huxley said.

"She thinks we're haunted, you mean?"

That was my understanding, more or less. I hadn't used the word, exactly.

I said maybe there was something to it. Perhaps we'd upset some kind of balance.

"Jesus, Jim. You've been acting strange for weeks."

"Have I?"

"Since the girl got here. I thought at first it was just having a new ass around that was driving you up the walls. New skin. I thought, ordinary enough, his blood's still pumping. But don't tell me you're going around town visiting psychics. Our beach house isn't haunted. Bruce isn't dead. Camille got tired of screwing Rami and took off. These things happen. People just go sometimes. They're not worried about what everybody else is going to think when they're gone. They just follow their impulses. They do as they please. You should try it sometime. Try not worrying about the others."

"That's not who I'm worried about."

"Of course you are. You're talking about the balance of a house. About ghosts."

I didn't want to argue. It felt like we were headed that way, and it was her last night before going. She would take a cab to the train station in the morning. I told her I would drive her, but she said it wasn't worth all the bother. It was simpler, just calling in a car.

After she was done packing, she opened the window and lit a joint. I didn't know where the joint had come from, but it seemed she had been keeping it somewhere nearby, maybe in the bedside table. She offered me some and we stood there in the window smoking and listening to birds over the marsh. They were making a racket about something, squawking back and forth. Maybe it had to do with food, or with mating. The truth is, I knew very little about what went on in that marsh, though I had lived beside it, at least for a season at a time, for the better part of my life, since age sixteen.

"I was trying to pick a fight before," she said.

Yes, I told her. I knew that she was. Fair enough. I was talking about ghosts.

She breathed out slowly. "I don't know why I wanted to do that. Probably because I'm leaving. It feels like I'm going to leave and come back, and everything will be different."

"Nothing will. Why would it be?"

"You'll scare them off, for one thing. You and your ghosts."

"Maybe I'll bring Miss Huxley in for another séance. Let her do the scaring."

"Tell me honestly: Did you fuck her, while she was here?"

"Miss Huxley?"

She elbowed me in the ribs, lightly. She was still looking out at the marsh. "No, you didn't, did you? What are we gonna do, Jim? You never take anything just for yourself."

The joint was finished, but she was still holding it as it burned down.

I told her about what Rami mentioned to me the other day on the beach, after finding that Camille had gone. The argument they had had. The fight he had dreamed about. How disturbed he seemed by it, even going so far as to ask about diplomatic immunity.

I thought she would have heard it already, but she hadn't, not even a hint of it.

"It's his conscience," she said. "He's feeling guilty. Next comes the wallowing."

"Guilty, why?"

"For sleeping with a woman who was supposed to be sleeping with his friend."

"I thought you were in favor of it."

She shook her head. "I only said it was bound to happen. It was an observation, from the start. Now he's feeling guilty, so what? He'll forget about it in a few days, forgive himself, then move on to some other affair. It was all fate—bound to play out this way."

"I think he went into it naively."

"You're projecting."

"You didn't talk to him on the beach. He was disturbed."

"He's not used to dreaming about killing someone. He's never been married."

"Do you dream about killing me?"

She bumped me this time with her hip, but it felt less playful than before, or else I was thinking only about the fact that we were in the window that way, and that watching the birds circle around in the moonlight was making me slightly dizzy. Or it was the weed.

I thought maybe she was going to remind me: She hardly ever remembered her dreams.

It was just that one time: her swimming off like a squid as Bruce drowned in front of her.

Then a sound began, slowly, but gathering a kind of momentum. At first it wasn't clear where the sound was coming from. I realized it was inside the house, and soon after it occurred to me that it was Shannon and Maya. Valentina was listening to it too. Probably she had known what it was from the first sound, and it had only taken me time to catch up. She smiled and said she was glad they were enjoying themselves still, six months in.

"Make sure they don't leave while I'm gone," she said.

Why would that be an issue? Nobody was going anywhere. Yet it was on her mind.

"I never know what to do with your friends," she said. "I like them all so much. I love them, I suppose. But you get different when they're around. It doesn't happen all at once. It grows. I look at you some nights and it's like you've run off and sent a replacement. Like you're trying to trick me. Don't listen to me. I'm getting pretty high."

She had managed to get one final puff out of the joint, then threw it down into the yard.

It seemed to me a reckless thing to do, but really there was no danger in it. There was a small patio down there, which we never used. The joint fell harmlessly onto the stone slabs, and she asked whether I wanted to sleep with the window open or closed. We had been sleeping with it open all summer and I thought it was an odd thing to ask that night, but maybe she was thinking of being discreet, thinking it was what I would want.

It was half an hour later, and I was still awake, when she spoke again.

The noises down the hall had stopped. The house had that sudden silence.

"It's not that you're awful around your friends," she said. "You're not obnoxious. It's nothing, really. But sometimes I feel like you've been keeping something from me, something big, and that everyone is in on it, like you've all agreed that I shouldn't be told."

"Like what?" I asked. "What do you mean, something big?"

"Like you were married before, and it ended badly. I thought that for a while."

"I didn't know that."

"I was sure you'd had some ugly divorce and all your friends had told you not to mention it to me, that it would scare me off. I kept expecting you to confess it finally. Confess all the ugly things you had done to one another. How it got so bad as all that."

"I was never married before."

"I know that now. Your parents were dead. That's what it was."

"But I told you that. From the beginning."

"No, you didn't."

"I must have. Of course I did."

"Do you really think so? Two days before the wedding—that was the first time."

I tried remembering the conversation. Remembering what I had told her up until then.

It was possible. In fact, she was probably right. Why had I withheld that?

"I'm sorry I didn't tell you sooner," I said. "I never realized I hadn't. Until now."

She was breathing slowly. I thought for a moment that she'd fallen asleep. Or that perhaps she was gathering her strength for something else: another thing I'd forgotten.

Sometimes you think these things—disputes, discrepancies—have been averted, but they're only lying in wait. You feel them coming for days before they actually emerge.

"It doesn't matter," she said. "I figured it all out on my own."

"What do you mean?"

"I asked your friends. You had done this bizarre thing and told them all different pieces of it. None of them got exactly the same or the whole story. Or the timing would be different. You were fifteen or you were sixteen. All these little changed details, which meant nothing. Or, I don't know, you told it to them at different points in your life, explaining, remembering it inconsistently. But you didn't tell any of them how it was."

"How they died, you mean."

"I had to look it up. I found some newspaper clippings, in the end."

"It was a fire."

"I know, Jim. We don't have to talk about it now. I figured it all out eventually."

"You read about it, you mean."

"Yes, I read about it."

There was a long silence, during which I put several ugly thoughts out of mind.

It was late, and she needed to sleep. Her cab was coming early, at six-thirty, so that she could beat some of the traffic to the train station. On weekdays, you never knew when there would be a great crush of people suddenly deciding to move around the coastline.

25

n the morning, I proposed to Rami that we clear brush from the yard. It took a few hours, and the physical labor seemed to do us both some good. Afterward, Maya brought the wheelbarrow around, since we hadn't given any thought as to what we were going to do with the branches once they were gathered. We carted them to a clearing near the edge of the marsh, and there was a vague notion between us, or at least forming in me, that we would build a bonfire, soon as conditions allowed. The beach was rather littered too. The tide had swept in mounds of algae and a smack of jellyfish. The twins insisted on getting a closer look and spent the better part of the day approaching, then retreating from, various specimens. There were dozens of them just on our stretch of beach. Some were as small as marbles. Others were the size of softballs.

While we were working, Rami came across a dead bird. An osprey, a full-grown male. You found animals around the marsh sometimes, birds especially. Usually they were small birds, and occasionally they'd lost their heads to a fisher cat. Rami asked if it was an omen and I told him no, that was only when they shit on you, and he said that was right, he remembered now. He must have been thinking about that ride in from the ferry, when we were in the Jeep with Bruce and the birds were overhead, following us. He asked if we should bury the osprey. I thought it better to leave the meat for coyotes.

That night I was feeling somewhat out of sorts and was mostly keeping my own company after dinner. There were lots of books around the house, but for some reason I picked out, from all of them, one of Bruce's, an old paperback that was lying around. I took it into the library and was thinking I would pass an hour with it before bed when the phone rang. It took me a moment to recognize the voice as belonging to one of my second cousins, Brett Pastore, and another moment after that to remember he worked for the district attorney. He began the conversation somewhat offhandedly, as though he called up the house quite regularly at that hour, just to catch me up on the day's events.

Brett and I were contemporaries, roughly speaking, but he always addressed me like he had some hard-earned homespun wisdom to bestow. He had been working as a prosecutor since law school and was now the chief of the office, the DA's top deputy.

He asked after Valentina and the twins and the house, but it was clear there was something else he'd called about, and he was eager to be done with these pleasantries.

"Listen, Jim," he said, when they were through. "Something has come up. I wanted to run it by you, take your temperature, try seeing what kind of sense it makes before it goes further. You understand how these things get around. I figured it'd be better to have a conversation first. Just us. It's nothing official. It's just a friendly chat, in family."

He was rambling somewhat. "What's it about, Brett? You've got me in suspense."

"The kids who broke into the Canham house. And the Belling-hams. The squatters."

I told him I'd heard about them: the kids, the break-ins, the arrest. All the local gossip.

"But what does it have to do with me?"

I asked quite innocently, but no sooner were the words out of my mouth than I remembered the encounter with Tom Shaw at the gro-cery store: how I had insisted, without any particular reason, that our house had never been broken into. I was wondering whether I was going to have to unspool that same lie with Brett, or take it further, when he stopped me. He explained there was one kid in particu-lar, the ringleader of the group. "One of those tough shits," Brett said, "who's seen too many movies and thinks he knows how it all works. He's got an attitude, like, fuck the world."

"All right," I said. "Are you handling the case?"

I could sense Brett shaking his head through the phone lines. He had always been somewhat jowly, but it was more the way he breathed that let you know how he was reacting. "Not mine," he said. "One of our girls is on it. Two days out of Suffolk Law, so they gave her a tres-pass. Doesn't matter, though. The point is about the kid. The defen-dant. Jeremy Schiller's his name. It took us a few days to square that one away."

I remembered now that Tom had mentioned the kids weren't car-rying IDs.

"That name," Brett said. "Schiller. It doesn't ring any bells? Take your time, think."

No, it didn't. I didn't see why it should.

"Because he's telling our people you're his lawyer."

"That I am?"

"You. To anyone who'll listen, he's been telling it."

"But that doesn't make any sense."

"He won't say more. Just that you're his attorney. Only he adds a little extra smart-ass into it whenever he mentions the name, like he knows you're not really . . ."

He trailed off, and I thought it best to finish for him.

"That I'm not a real lawyer."

"That you don't practice."

"I never got licensed in Massachusetts to begin with."

"Like he knows it's a joke. Anyway, I wanted to run it by you first, check it out."

"I wish I could explain it."

That wish hung between us for a time. I imagined him running a hand through his hair.

He told me not to worry about it. He had never believed it to begin with. Then he apologized for not coming by the house on the Fourth. He said he and Linda, his wife, would stop by one night for dinner. They hadn't stopped by for dinner in all the time I'd been in the house. I couldn't recall if he was one of the usual attendees of the party we threw on the Fourth, though he must have been, from the way he had mentioned it.

"Give my love to . . . everyone," he said.

He was searching for the names of my kids. Or maybe he knew we had guests.

After we hung up, I tried going back to reading but couldn't make any heads or tails of it. It was a book I had read before, years back, but the plot seemed to me almost entirely new, or like it was something I had heard described secondhand. I was thinking, maybe, of the story about those kids and the break-ins as relayed to me by Tom Shaw.

I decided to call Valentina. I wanted to tell her what had happened, but when I finally got her on the line, I didn't know quite what to say and ended up telling her instead about the tide and the jellyfish that had washed up on the beach, tangled in the algae.

The whole reason for calling her was to tell her about that conversation with Brett. She was good about things like that, reasoning them all the way through, discerning the motivations behind people's odd behavior. But soon, I let her go without getting into it.

It sounded like she was busy. I could hear people talking in the background. Dishes were clanging about. Voices were chattering. I figured they were having a late dinner.

26

The Patuxet jail had none of the usual New England gloom hanging around it, no sense of displacement or disharmony, no feeling that witches had been burned nearby the grounds. It wasn't even built from a basement, as most village jails are in that part of the country. Nearly all civil functions save the harbormaster's were run out of the same strip of rambling, shingled buildings one block uphill from the pier, and I liked to imagine it gave some of the inhabitants of those offices and cells, indentured or otherwise, hope to be so near the ferry landing and to hear the boat's horn sounding twice daily. I had never spent much time around the building except for two weeks when I first took possession of the house: I had roamed between various clerks all hours of the day, petitioning for documents. A deputy surveyor finally took pity on me and advised it was the local custom—obsequious, maybe, but effective—for a new owner in my position, wishing for a smooth entry, to buy a half-gallon box of coffee from the Dunkin' Donuts on Agawam and to carry it around, along with cups and creams and sweeteners, to be able to offer the clerks something there on the spot. It did the job and got me out of the building with all my permits in a matter of hours. Since that time, I had always felt like I was in a sympathetic position with the town bureaucracy, as though we understood one another on a fundamental level and had long ago made the necessary accommodations. In any case it must have been the reason why I decided to stop for coffee on my way to the jail that next morning. Even in that somewhat more guarded environment, the trick worked well. I was accepted as a certified attorney who had every right to pay one of his clients a visit.

I was shown into a small room painted in aquamarine hues and waited there for twenty minutes before the guard reappeared, now accompanying a young man who was not restrained or cuffed. They were talking quietly about something, then stopped as they entered the room. The young man was tall, at least six three or four, and carried himself rigidly. He had some faint acne scarring across one cheek but otherwise his complexion and coloring were immaculate and gave him the air of an overgrown child.

"Oh, hello," he said, coming into the room. "It's good of you to see me."

I thought he was approaching to shake hands. He had that open, welcoming expression on his youthful face, but instead he only sat down across from me at the table and smiled expectantly and waited for the guard to leave us, which he soon did, with a nod.

It was early still. I had woken up at six and paced around the house for a while and made the kids breakfast, then left without telling anyone where I was headed. I wasn't quite resolved about it myself, except a part of me must have been because I took the Jeep and drove straight to the Dunkin' Donuts. I never liked starting the day in a car. It seemed to run contrary to local geography and to the pleasure of going about it on foot.

The room we were in had a barred window. From that vantage you could see that the town was just beginning to gain steam, and that the package store across the street was opening its doors. It wouldn't be able to sell anything but lottery and scratch tickets for another two hours, until noon came around. That was a local ordinance. I wondered what kind of cell they were holding the kid in and whether it, too, had views of the street. Had he seen me coming out of the package store with my wagon full of wine and liquor? Although that wouldn't have explained anything, really. It wouldn't have made sense of him giving my name to the DA's office and calling me his lawyer.

"I heard I'm representing you," I said.

The kid smiled. "It really was good of you to come."

"You said that already."

"You are a lawyer, aren't you?"

"Not here, I'm not. I'm licensed in New York and Connecticut, and barely that."

"Oh," he said, not sounding disappointed or flummoxed, but like he was merely processing new information. He held, it was clear from that brief exchange, a high opinion of his own intellect. I had no reason to doubt it either. He had, anyway, a kind of composure not often come across in everyday settings. It wasn't arrogance, not quite.

"How old are you?" I asked.

"Twenty," he said. Then, with a new breath, he corrected himself. "Nineteen, actually."

"And you told the police and the DA's office that I was your lawyer."

"Yes."

"Any particular reason?"

"They arrested us."

He wasn't trying to be coy. He seemed to think the matter self-explanatory.

"Look," he said, leaning in. "You should call me Billy, if that's all right."

"Your name's not Jeremy? They told me that was how you were processed."

He breathed in heavily. It wasn't quite a sigh. "It is. But I prefer Billy. Is that all right?"

His hands were on the desk in front of him, folded neatly. They were delicate hands, and for some reason that delicacy made me question part of the story I had been told by my cousin. This was the ringleader? Squatting, it seemed to me, was labor intensive, arduous. Not something any kid off the street with a smirk and a haircut could pull off.

"Here's the thing," he said. "I'm a little worried."

"I would imagine you might be."

"They arrested us for aggravated trespassing. Okay, fair enough. We don't recognize traditional property laws or values. It's inherent in our lifestyle. Occasionally they're gonna lock us up somewhere. Understood. Once you're in, it's a matter of mindset. We were living somewhere we weren't meant to be. We're still living somewhere we're not meant to be. We like to be together, and in here, they don't keep us far apart. The rooms are all side by side. But if we have to stay here, wait for a trial or a plea or any of that, anything more than a few more days, they'll transfer us somewhere else. I'm sure of it."

"Yes, they will," I said. "I'm surprised they haven't transferred you already."

"And yet, here we are."

"But why am I here?"

I felt, once the words were out, somewhat more exposed. Like he knew I was wondering the answer of myself, more than of him. I often give myself away like that.

He smiled and leaned forward closer still. I could smell citrus on his breath.

Had they given him juice that morning? A good breakfast in the cells? Probably, yes.

"How old are you?" he asked.

"Thirty-eight."

"That's two of me."

"How's that?"

"Two of me. You've been around longer. Had time to sort things. People know you here. They listen to you. More so because you leave again—the end of summer, right? There's a power in that sort of thing. Leaving, when it suits you, when seasons change. What I want—we want—is to be on our way: to go. Ideally before charges are revisited."

Here he leaned in farther, and in that pose, which wasn't confiding, exactly, but seemed merely another way of holding himself rigid, he reminded me of Bruce. Bruce as he had been once. As I had known him, when we first met and formed the basis for our friendship. That odd mix of self-sustenance and urgent need, which began with the need to explain himself in oblique, fleeting terms and for me somehow to understand.

It occurred to me, also, to wonder whether the kid might be crazy. It was entirely possible, though I didn't think so, and if I had it wouldn't really have changed anything. I was still there. He had summoned me. I was still wondering why he had.

"Why would the charges be revisited?" I asked.

A smile formed at his lips, then cut itself off before it could develop fully.

"Well," he said, "the thing is, we've had, also, some fires."

I waited for him to explain. Or perhaps he was going to give over to the smile.

"There may be some fires in our wake, if they follow the trail back, I mean."

"You've burned things? Arson?"

"How do I explain this? It's part of the lifestyle. You know when people go camping, and there's a policy, whatever you bring into a forest, you bring out again? Or people who compost. Underlying it is a principle: We ought to remove our traces, if possible."

"I think it's more about cleanliness. Consideration."

"Consideration for others, you think?" There was scorn in his voice, but only a sliver.

"But what have you burned?"

"Well, we were here, in the area, for most of the spring. Right up and through until, say, May, which is when we moved to the Canham house. Before that, we tended to build fires as we left, to get rid of what we'd used. And also, whenever possible, the houses."

It took a moment to understand what he was saying. He wanted me to wonder, I think.

"You burned the houses?"

"Right, as a gesture, when we left."

"But you can't have."

"Why not?" He seemed really to want to know.

"I mean, it would be known. This is a small town. You can't be a serial arsonist."

He scoffed now. The scorn he had been holding in before was let loose, finally. "You know, your generation. You think you understand the world perfectly because you've been around a few years but haven't started shitting yourself quite yet. But you will start, you've already started. We're the only ones who can smell it. That's how it goes."

He closed his eyes and opened them again. It was a slow, deliberate movement.

Then he went on. "Look, I didn't ask you here to argue. You're a lawyer. I know how that'll turn out. I won't win. I'm just asking you to think over how you might be able to help us, okay? That's all I want. I know this has been a backward way of asking for it."

"You're asking for my consideration."

"That's right," he said appreciatively. "You see that? A lawyer's trick, right? Turning the words back on me. Would you meet with my friends, do you think? You don't have to. They've agreed to let me speak on behalf of the group. But if you wanted to meet them, that would be all right. They could tell the guards that you're their lawyer too. The girls are nice. I told them about you, and they'd like to meet you. Anytime, really."

"No, Billy, I don't want to meet them."

"Are you sure?"

"I'm not sure what I'm doing here to begin with."

"You were curious. Aren't you curious to meet them? You came all this way."

"It wasn't far."

"I only mean, you took the time. A morning of your life, so why not?"

"I'm going to go," I said.

"All right."

"Don't use my name again. Whatever this is, drop it. Don't list me on any forms."

"If you change your mind, we'll be here."

"Yes, you're in jail."

"They won't transfer us for a few days still, I think. In case you want to come."

I felt suddenly, and perhaps a bit belatedly, that he was offering something. That I was talking to a pimp, in short. Why I should have been so sure that was what he was implying, I couldn't explain, but the feeling overcame me, and I stood up from where I was sitting and went over to the window and wanted to be outside again. The air in there felt serrated and suffocating and I wanted to be outside, to expel it from my lungs.

I called for the guard but found it wasn't necessary. They had never locked the door to begin with. A few moments later I was back outside and absorbed into the morning of the village center. I walked back by the window where we had met and saw the kid was still sitting inside, there at the table. The guard who had shown me in was with him, holding a cup of coffee from the half-gallon box I had brought along, and he had poured a cup of it for the kid as well, and they were both looking dreamily out the window, enjoying their drinks, neither one paying me much mind as I passed them by.

would have liked to bring the matter, strange as it was, to Valentina, but she was still entangled in the scandal back in New Haven, on campus. She wasn't picking up or responding to my texts. Rami wanted to get lunch out, and I told him I would go along.

We went to the same restaurant, on the deck in back of the taffy shop, hanging out over the pier, where we had gone to talk over Camille leaving, only this time I was the one searching for words, trying to sound almost careless about the thing, though in the end I more or less came out with it and told him where I had been that morning and who I had spoken with and why. I was struggling to make some connection to earlier events, to that vague sensation I had been wrestling with for the last few weeks, that something strange had transpired, and it had to do with the house and our stay, which felt to me in some fashion compromised, like I had bungled something quite important from the very start. Yet I didn't mention anything to him about going back to see Miss Huxley or about what she thought of Camille. It wouldn't have made any sense and would have caused him grief to talk about her that way, like an abstraction. She wasn't a spirit, or a force. She was the woman who had most recently left him, with a rather baffling suddenness, without even leaving a note. It would have seemed like I was teasing him.

"What I don't understand," Rami said, "is why this kid, Billy or Jeremy, picked you. There are plenty of lawyers around here. Vacation lawyers, if that's his preference."

"There's one reason I can think of."

"All right, what is it?"

"He was in our house."

It was the only explanation I could come up with, and not a wholly satisfying one at that, which I readily admitted, but it was my belief, half-formed until I gave it words, that he and his friends had spent some portion of the spring, or perhaps all of it, living in our house. That was the meaning of summoning me the way he had, and of the various hints he was trying to drop during our conversation. It had to be that.

"Okay," Rami said. "So they squatted there. He knows about you, from the inside."

"He knows something about me, in that case. About us."

"Something embarrassing?"

"I don't know. It's hard to say what he was after."

An eyebrow raised. "Blackmail—is that what you're thinking. Christ, Jim. Why? How?"

"It could be something more innocent than that. Or not. Or he wanted me to understand that I'd been violated. That he had done the violating and could do more."

"Or he just wanted somebody to talk to."

"Yes," I admitted. "That's possible too."

"People in trouble do it all the time, don't they? Clutch at straws.

Write letters to anybody with an address. They're fishing, trying to find somebody who might help."

We weren't getting anywhere. It wasn't his fault, but I wished Valentina were there too.

"Should you be telling me any of this?" he asked.

"What do you mean?"

"You're not bound by any ethical concerns?"

He was right, of course. The kid had named me as his attorney. Whether I could lawfully serve the function or not, I was meant to pretend, and to keep his secrets.

Still, we went on. There was really no point in holding back, ethics notwithstanding.

"Assume your suspicion is right," Rami said. "The kid was in your house. He had access, for what it's worth. But that's the question: What is it worth? What could he possibly be hoping to blackmail you with? You don't just leave dark, incriminating secrets around your beach house in the offseason, do you? Or is there a vault around?"

"There's nothing, really."

"Then there you go."

"It's just a feeling . . ."

He was waiting for me to finish. Our fish was getting cold.

"That he's been watching us," I said. "In the time since."

"Watching us?"

"Haven't you had that feeling at all this summer? That we're somehow on display?"

He thought it over for a time. He always treated seriously what you hoped he would.

"It's because Camille was around," he said. "She was a stranger. Watching us."

"Probably that's it."

"And if he had been watching us, what would he have seen? You're feeling guilty."

I agreed. I was, and likely that was the source of my confusion. But why should I?

To that, he didn't have an answer. We ate in silence for a time and walked home along the beach, stopping twice to skip rocks. He had gotten quite good at it. I wondered if he had been practicing. He had such a smooth, easy motion now, whereas before it had seemed to me the mechanics of the gesture, if not its significance, were a mystery to him.

———◦———

After I put the kids to bed, I came back downstairs and found that Rami had taken it on himself to explain to Maya and Shannon all about my encounter that morning at the jail.

"I don't like it," Maya said. "It's creepy. All of it."

She had a glass of rum in her hands, gripped tightly.

"I don't like it either," I said. "That's why I went to see him. If he's using my name, I want to know why. If he was here, in the house, I want to know the details—when or what he wants to get out of it now. I'm in the dark on this one, as much as anybody is."

Shannon was the only one who seemed wholly unconcerned. She said the kid was nineteen. "Do you remember all the stupid ideas we had when we were nineteen?"

I appreciated that question. It sounded to me almost exactly like one Valentina would have posed. And in fact, after we had all discussed it some more, I went upstairs and tried her on the phone once again. I got the idea in my head that it might have something to do with my phone, so I asked Rami to borrow his and half expected her to pick up. Why that would be the case, I can't say, but anyway, she didn't. It just rang through and eventually told me her voicemail was full. I sent another text from my phone and waited up a while, but when I went to sleep, she still hadn't read the thing.

I wasn't too concerned, really. She was working. It was always like that once she locked on to a problem. Her attention was like a clamp. It was one of the things you admired about her, and if she didn't manage to check in every day, you knew exactly why it was.

Still, I must have been unsettled because I woke up twice in the night and ran a quick inspection of the halls, thinking I had heard the sound of water running, which it may have been, through the pipes. I wanted to understand what it was, why it was so loud.

Nothing turned up, and on the second run-through I went downstairs and saw Maya sitting out on the porch. She was in almost precisely the position I had been that first night after we had arrived, when I was sitting with that harpoon, watching the marsh.

"Can't sleep?" I asked.

She didn't turn to me immediately. She was wearing a long robe that hung open, and I felt rather like I had snuck up on her and seen something that I shouldn't have. But when she saw me, she didn't bother covering herself. Why should she have, really?

"It's been weeks," she said. "I wake up every night."

I told her I hadn't realized it. I had never seen or heard her up and about the house.

"This is the first time I've gotten up," she said. "It's Shannon. She rolls around all night trying to find the right position. And she has that pillow. That snake. It's like she's wrestling with it. I'm lying there just waiting to find out who'll win. I hate that thing."

"It's just a few months," I said. "After the birth, she can sleep on her stomach again."

She turned, with something new in her eye. Distrust, maybe, or something worse.

"It's none of your goddamn business how we sleep," she said.

"Of course. I'm sorry. We don't have to talk about it."

"It's nobody's goddamn business but our own. Why can't everybody just accept that?"

She shifted her weight and her robe fell farther open. She noticed it now and cinched it.

"Go to bed," she said. "I've had too much to drink. I'll feel better in the morning."

I began to do that when she called me back. There was something else.

"That bird," she said. "The one Rami found. It's still out there."

"The osprey?"

"You said the coyotes would take it."

"They should have."

"Well, it's still there. I saw it. Couldn't you bury it? It's disturbing, having it there."

Yes, I told her, I would take care of it. I was sorry not to have done it sooner.

I felt compelled then to tell her, also, about my worries over the house, and about the feeling that we had been watched. By Camille, maybe, the squatters, or somebody else.

It was such a strong urge to speak, to put the idea into words, but the words wouldn't come, and I felt more foolish for being inarticulate. It was a kind of hysteria pumping through my veins. That's how it felt. I could have imagined just then any number of untoward things. Maybe it was the landscape that inspired it. It had inspired all manner of madness before. I looked out at the marsh and had precisely that thought before leaving. On the way upstairs, I promised myself I really would do something about the osprey, soon as there was light, assuming the coyotes didn't come around to take it first.

The coyotes, in their hunger, were clever, and would never show themselves when or how you expected them to. They would come at such odd times, then disappear again.

28

t was Friday before I went back to the jail. Part of me hoped they would have shipped the kid and his friends off to Bridgewater or released them on bail. I didn't call ahead and didn't bring coffee this time, but they let me in anyway and seemed perfectly pleasant about it. They gave us the same room as before. Billy came breezing in a few minutes later. Again, there were no cuffs. He had that very assured manner of approaching, and the smile on his face suggested he had been expecting I would return.

I wasn't in a hostile mood, yet I wanted to get into it, so we didn't bother with any pleasantries. I asked whether he and his friends had been in my house. Is that what it was all about? It would be better if he would just come out and explain himself, finally.

He was nodding very thoughtfully as I spoke and seemed to be making an effort to knit his brow, but it struck me as an unnatural gesture, like he'd read somewhere this was how a man behaved when he wanted the person he was speaking with to feel heard. The nodding went on for some time before he answered. His voice was rather gentle.

"Well, yes," he said. "We were there. But not for long. Only one night, actually, then we moved on. This was April, I think. I am sorry.

I didn't know it was your house at the time. It could have been any-body's house. It's a good-looking place, and big too. With that roof, which is what drew me to it. I like architecture, the theory more than the practice. All that hidden significance. I figured there would be food around for us too."

He sounded like he thought I had come to interview him. Like I was with the paper.

"But it was only a night," he said. "I'm sorry if we broke anything. It was happening fast. Moving in, then out. Was there any damage? I hope we didn't cause you trouble."

Again, he struck me as someone who had studied the emotions he was hoping to convey: in this case, a bizarre kind of contrition whose purpose I really didn't grasp.

"So should I file a report? Since we're in agreement about what happened."

"You didn't file one then? I didn't think you had. You see, we didn't like the place."

"You didn't like it?"

"It didn't like us. That can happen too. So we had to get out. I'm sure you understand."

I didn't understand. He seemed to be waiting to explain himself.

"You must get used to it, and I suppose, well, it's been in your fam-ily a long time."

"Get used to what?"

"The noises. The . . . appearances. We're an open-minded group. That's one of our principles. To claim you have all the answers about what's here and what's not, what comes before and what comes after, that's arrogance. Extremism, under another name."

He was about to launch into a speech, I was sure. He was gathering his breath.

"What exactly appeared to you in my house?" I asked.

His eyes narrowed. He was trying to decide whether I was serious.

"Normally we burn the houses after we leave," he said. "But of course there was no time, and even if there had been, I wouldn't have been too inclined, given everything."

"Burned my house, you mean?"

"That's right."

"Your story doesn't make any sense, Billy."

Hearing his name, his real name or one he had given himself, seemed to take him aback.

"What do you mean, my story?"

"You've been squatting around since April, or before. And burning places as you leave. Where's the evidence? Where are the arsons? You think in a small town like this people don't know when a house burns down? Either you're full of shit, crazy, or a bit of both."

"But you came back to see me again. That was good of you. We went to see you too."

He wanted me to ask what he meant. I held back, believing he would say it anyway.

"On the Fourth," he said. "At your party. We came and built a fire on the beach, and I watched all of you. You had a fight with your friend, in the water. The big guy, I don't know his name, but he was staying with you. You were wrestling around in the water like a pair of walruses. I almost stepped in, but it seemed like you needed to do it."

The room suddenly felt cold. I was caught out, of course, but then, what did it matter?

"There were a lot of people there that night," I said.

Yes, he agreed, there were. Apparently, he and his friends were among them.

What of it? We sat in silence for a minute or two, some unnaturally long period.

Then he said, "We had been arrested once by then already. Once here, I mean. We've been arrested other places, but that was the first time around here. We were out again."

Yes, I told him. I had heard about their arrest. News gets around in a place like Patuxet.

"But you didn't turn us away," he said. "You gave us a meal. Welcomed us back."

"I wouldn't have, if I'd known."

"No?"

"I would have called the police."

"That's the night I talked with the French woman. There were so many people there."

He was watching now, to see how I would react.

"The French woman?"

"I didn't know if she was staying with you or had just shown up, like us."

"Describe her, Billy."

He smiled and offered up something very neutral, the kind of thing you might say to describe almost any woman you'd come across on the street. The words meant nothing.

"And she was there on the Fourth?"

"It was when you were fighting that I met her. She was watching you too. She told me to build the fire because it was getting cool and people would want a fire to warm up."

I was getting angry, but there was no point in giving the kid any kind of satisfaction.

"You didn't meet her that night," I said. "She wasn't there that night, Billy. Your timeline is off. Whatever con you're trying to run on me—on us—get your facts straight."

"That's the thing," he said. "It wasn't the first time I met her. I realized it after."

He leaned toward me again. I saw a flash of something in his eyes. Madness, maybe.

"She was one of them I saw in the house. When we stayed there. I knew her already."

"In my house?"

"Don't you see? Maybe you can't, because you think it's yours. She was there already. And then we got to talking again that night, on the Fourth. About the fire, while we watched you fight, and then when you were done, again later, she came over and gave me some tips about how to keep it burning longer. She showed me how to stack the wood. She said I should build one closer to the house too. There were people up there."

It wasn't madness in his eyes. He was looking at me as he had once before, with scorn.

The silence lasted some time. I wasn't going to ask him another question.

I wasn't going to ask him anything at all, though I wanted to. The hell with him, all of it.

"I want you to stop telling people I'm your lawyer," I said. "Don't try to contact me. Scrounge up bail money, or don't. It doesn't matter to me. I'm going to withdraw as your attorney. If I even need to do it. We'll go back to being strangers. We never met."

The scorn was all you could read on him now. It was like he couldn't stand to be in the room with me. "All right," he said. "Sure. I figured you wouldn't really want to hear it."

He got up and walked out. The guards didn't seem concerned. I doubt they'd ever had a serious breakout attempt. Billy certainly wasn't going to be their first.

29

We were having such a good night, and after dinner, after the kids went upstairs, Shannon found the coffee tin that held the pennies and we all sat down at the kitchen table to play cards. I could see their faces so clearly, as they had been twenty years before, and all the game's lies, bluffs, and bluster fooled me so completely, I couldn't begin to fathom which card I had on my forehead or where I stood against any of them. It was a wonderful mystery. I went to the pantry and found we were out of the green wine, then remembered that I had stored more of it in the shed outside. The wine was warm, so we drank it over ice. Yet it felt like one of those evenings when no compromises need be made, when the world will provide whatever you might wish for.

I thought about telling them what had been said at the jail. The story was turning over in my mind for a time, and I was thinking how best to present it in an acceptable form but couldn't land on any one version that would play how I thought it ought to, so I kept it to myself. It could wait until morning. Any number of things could wait until morning, and we were in no rush. It was the first time all summer I could remember that nobody said they were tired or ought to get to bed. It takes only a hint of that sort of thing—a look shared between two people who believe they're unobserved—and the night's done. We were getting drunk and there was no room for subtlety or obfuscation.

Rami began telling a story about something that happened in Budapest. It wasn't the story about the German woman he got pregnant. It was something else entirely. He had, one day, played hooky when he was meant to be leading a breakout session on grain duties. He hadn't been able to bear the thought of going to work and came up with an illness that would excuse him without derailing negotiations. He went to the park instead and was thinking about falling asleep in a chair, in the sun, when he saw a woman kneel to the ground, before going prostrate. She was having a seizure, it turned out.

When he went to her, she took his hand. She was trembling. The convulsions gathered strength, then soon leveled into something softer. He said it was almost like she was sleeping, after a time. All this unfolded over thirty or forty seconds, but there were distinct periods to it, and when it was done, before any more help arrived, before an ambulance could reach them, the woman merely stood up, brushed the dirt from her clothes, and said something to him. It was in Hungarian, so he didn't know what she said, but he decided immediately, and became convinced later on, that it was a blessing.

"And I've been walking around with that blessing ever since," he said.

"Have you really?" Shannon asked. She seemed so delighted with the prospect.

"Yes, and to tell you the truth, I wonder every day whether I'm squandering it."

"But maybe," I said, "it was just her saying thank you. Or telling you to let the ambulance go, sorry about the trouble. Or she was explaining it happens all the time."

He wasn't having any of it. He was as convinced of the blessing as the day it arrived.

"The point is," he said, "two days later, I decided to take my holiday, to come here. Before that, before the woman in the park, I was thinking I would go to the mountains. I had this stupid idea I was going to climb a mountain somewhere alone, or at least a good-sized hill, and I would find the highest cabin they could build and stay there a week. I had bought these shoes for it already. Sneakers. The kind you climb hills in."

He raised his glass of green wine, proposing a toast.

"I needed to see you all," he said. "That was the blessing. I'm glad we're here."

Maya was crying, listening to the story, or to its culmination. When she saw the faces turned toward her, she waved off the attention and began laughing and said it was nothing, just tears, just this, meaning her glass of rum. When we were younger, she used to cry every time she got drunk. It hadn't happened in years, maybe since college, but there had been a time when not a weekend would pass without her weeping. The odd, lovely thing was, she never seemed sad or like she was crying about any particular thing, good or bad. It was some private feeling that she would sit with for a time and indulge.

The card game had been interrupted by the story, but we soon picked it up again.

Shannon was the only one who wasn't drunk, and as the game went on we were all laughing and Maya was crying occasionally and Shannon began to win all the hands.

"What am I going to do with all these pennies?" she said. If you looked at her or at the pennies for too long, she would throw out her arms like they were a treasure in need of guarding. She had never, in my estimation, been more beautiful. Her hair had that lovely copper tint. I felt I couldn't be the only one who was noticing, especially as she threw her arms out that way and lowered her chin to just a few inches above the coins, some of which were showing signs of age and storage, but the others were gleaming.

We took our drinks and moved to the living room. Maya sat down on the floor with a cushion beneath her. Her head was resting against Rami's leg, and her arm was draped across Shannon's lap. I got up to fill a carafe of water. It seemed such a responsible measure, and I was feeling proud for having thought of it when I noticed something outside, through the window behind the sink. A coyote had come onto the lawn. I didn't recognize him. You could see his ribs, the way he was seated, facing squarely toward the house, a calmness in his eyes, like he had made up his mind what needed doing. Beside him was the osprey carcass, the one I had promised to get rid of, if the coyotes didn't take it first. All this was illuminated vaguely by the light from the kitchen. Why didn't he take the carcass away with him? He could drag it off if he tried.

It didn't seem to interest him. He was interested, just then, in holding my gaze, and nothing else. Then something spooked him, and he ran off into the darkness. I waited a moment more. The water was still running. I had left the tap open to get cold and it was still going, but I didn't think of it, because something else had grabbed my attention. Something flashing suddenly from the darkness outside the kitchen light: a movement.

I didn't know what it was, but my first thought was that it was a

body. A person, running. Something big enough to scare off the coyote that had appeared so poised.

A trick of the light. Of the darkness. Something the mind detects
but can't define.

I filled the carafe and went back to the living room. I began to say
something about the coyote when Maya held out a hand and told me
to be quiet, for God's sake, just hold still. They were waiting for something, listening closely. Soon, it came: a tap at the glass.

"Where is that coming from?" I asked.

I knew which window it was coming from but for some reason had
wanted to ask.

"That's the third time," Maya said.

"The third time of what?"

"Something tapped against the window."

I hadn't heard it from the kitchen, though it was a sharp sound,
like metal. A ring, maybe. Maya got up from the cushion and began
pushing back the shades and curtains.

"Two taps," she said. "An accident, maybe. That's nothing. But
three . . ."

I was thinking we had all drunk too much. The water would do us
some good.

She wasn't having it. "Forget the water. I know what I heard."

It was nothing, I said. It was late. We should go to bed, or there'd
be hell to pay in the morning. We were already going to pay for it, but
some water and aspirin would help.

"Maybe it was a bird," Rami said. He sounded philosophical
about it.

And he may have been right. A beak, if it were hard enough, might
sound like metal.

Then the noise came again, this time from the kitchen. A moment later the phone rang.

"What the hell?" Maya said. "What's going on here?"

It was the landline. I had to think a moment where the receiver was. The ringing carried on, and I could feel them watching me. There was, it seemed, an accusation in the silence. I couldn't figure out the nature of it or what exactly they expected from me.

The phone was hanging on the wall in the kitchen, next to a corkboard. I picked it up but there was nobody on the line. Not even static. It was very quiet, and I got the impression there was nobody calling us. It had only been some kind of crazy mistake.

"What mistake?" Maya said. "You think the phone company's testing lines?"

"I don't know. I don't know anything about phone lines."

But she was watching me so closely, like she believed that I did know.

Rami, who may have been the drunkest of all of us, shrugged, began to formulate a thought, then abandoned it halfway to coherence. He reached for the carafe of water and poured out four glasses. He always filled other people's glasses before his own. It wasn't superstition but he believed very deeply in it. It wouldn't have mattered how drunk he was or how much at a loss, he never would have considered pouring one for himself alone if there were others around. I felt so grateful to him just then. It was such a delicate gesture, and it reminded me almost immediately of the grace with which he conducted himself at the baptism, all those years ago, in a Catholic church, of all places.

After he was done pouring and had handed the glasses all around and had taken his own, we held still for what seemed like such a long time, though it may have been a minute only, or not even that. The phone didn't ring again. There was no more tapping.

"It was nothing," I said. "It's over now. I'm feeling drunk."

Rami made the first move for the stairs. He had his water and was going to bed. He stopped on the first landing and turned back to us and gathered himself for a question.

"The kids," he said. "I was thinking, I don't know, I'd like to check on them, if that's all right. But then, I'm not sure if I'd wake them. Do you ever go into their room while they're sleeping, just to see them before you go to bed, but without waking them up?"

I told him it would be fine. Kids, they slept through almost anything. They might shift a little in their beds, but they wouldn't wake at his presence. Maybe other people's kids were different, but that's how ours were. And it touched me that he wanted to see them.

———◦———

I turned off the lights after the others had gone upstairs and poured myself another glass of water and picked up the rum that Maya had been working on for hours. Then I went outside and took up a position on the porch, in the same rocking chair where I'd sat vigil that first night, with the harpoon at my side. All around the house was darkness, but across the marsh a fire had been built. A camping fire, from the look of it.

It must have been burning in a clearing where the woods gave way to marsh. That was where the coyotes came from, but they wouldn't go anywhere near a fire, even for food.

A half hour later, Maya came outside. She had changed into pajamas.

"Jim," she said. "Be straight with me."

I thought about handing her the glass of rum, which I hadn't drunk from.

"I went back to talk with that kid at the jail today," I said.

"What did he want?"

"He said they squatted in the house. Earlier, before we came. Only for a night."

She seemed to be thinking carefully about what to say next, weighing her words.

"They stayed a night, and then what?"

I hesitated but didn't say anything, which was a sort of answer.

"Are they still locked up?" she asked.

"I assume so. I saw him this morning. They hadn't made bail yet."

"But you're wondering . . . whether he's come back?"

"Yes."

"The one kid, or all of them?"

"I don't know."

"To what? Fuck with us?"

"Maybe. I don't know."

"No, that's no fun. They want something."

I nodded. There was no point denying it. I was thinking, wondering all kinds of things.

"When the phone rang," I said, "my first thought: It's my cousin. The one at the DA's office. I was thinking he was going to tell me that the kids made bail, or the charges were dropped. He wouldn't call in the middle of the night like that, but that's what I was thinking." I made a gesture, directing her toward the marsh. Until that moment, she had been looking toward the beach but now she saw the fire, or I presumed she did.

"Are you going to stay here all night?" she asked.

"I don't know. It's nothing, I'm sure. At worst, some stupid kids."

She sat down in the daybed beside me and stretched her legs across the cushion.

I pushed the glass of rum closer to her, but she didn't appear to notice.

"You know we're having a boy," she said.

"No, I didn't know that."

She nodded. "We didn't mean to. We decided we didn't want to know the sex of the embryo, just whether it was healthy. We told them use the healthiest one, and we'll be surprised, but then one of those tests came back. There's a hundred of them: tests. Nobody tells you how goddamn many there are. They were supposed to hide the sex but forgot, so now we know. A boy. Who the hell knows what to do with a boy? How many ways there are to fuck them up. They don't get fucked up alone either. A girl might keep it to herself, but not a boy. If he's fucked up, he's going to make you feel it."

She was quiet for a time and still didn't reach for the rum.

"This kid," she said, "what did you say his name was?"

"Billy. Jeremy, but he goes by Billy."

"If he comes around here, I feel like I'm going to kill him."

She sounded more earnest, perhaps, than I had ever heard her.

"I've been feeling that, lately," she said. "It's strange. Like it would be nothing, something like that. Not nothing, but it wouldn't be a surprise. It would be almost ordinary and something I should've seen coming the whole time. Fucking hell, with that girl, too, it was like that. I thought, at first, I wanted to fuck her, but it wasn't that."

"Camille?"

"I would think about choking her. Have you ever done that?"

"No." For some reason, I didn't want to tell her about the time Valentina asked me to.

"Neither have I. So why was I thinking about it?"

"Well, she's gone now."

"But where did she go?"

"I don't know."

She nodded, as though that were her point, the one she had been coming around to.

"Shannon had this crazy idea," she said. "She wanted me to talk to the girl. Camille. Convince her to come back to Hudson with us. To help out when the baby comes. I don't know, an au pair, I guess. The kind you slip into bed with after the kid's asleep, get your exercise in, all your frustrations, your worries out, although she never spelled that out. She kept talking about it like it was this thing we would do. A gift we were giving each other, giving ourselves. It was nuts. The girl, she's a college professor. She lives in France. Why would she want to move in with two lesbians and their baby in fucking Hudson? But Shannon made it sound like, if I couldn't deliver this for her, for us, I was failing. Like it was the first test of us being parents: convincing, seducing her."

"I thought she wanted you to paint her."

That drew a laugh. A hard, bitter laugh. "The painting was meant to be for me."

"The painting and the choking."

"Right. Then she would move in. That was for both of us."

"And the baby."

"The baby too. All four of us."

We sat for a while as I tried thinking about what I wanted to tell her.

"If it's a boy," I said, "you won't fuck him up. It won't get that far. They're not that different, boys and girls. You think it's going to be a different experience altogether but they're just shitting and eating and sleeping. You learn to keep them alive until things reach an even keel, then years go by, and they hardly need you for anything, any of them. You go back to how you were before. You don't think about killing anybody."

"Is that how you are? Back to how you were before?"

"I think so."

"But sitting on the porch, in case the squatters come."

"They're not just squatters."

"What else?"

"Arsonists too. They have a set of principles."

"Jesus Christ, remember those? And how old, you said?"

"Nineteen, the leader."

"Fucking hell. This is too much, Jim. It was fun for a while, but it's too much now."

I hadn't even told her all of it. I was thinking of trying but didn't know how to start.

She seemed quite tired and still a little drunk.

"What about the kid in New York?" I asked.

She nodded, like we had both understood that was what we were talking about all along, or a part of it. We had always had that understanding between us, I believed.

Maybe that was why I didn't feel the need to spell it all out for her: about Camille.

"I think I used to babysit him," she said. "I've been coming around to it, and that's it. When I was a teenager, out on the Vineyard, probably. I used to run it like a business out there, summers. I babysat for everyone. Fourteen dollars an hour. It was a lot then."

"And he was one of the kids?"

"I think so. Grown up a bit. Twenty years later. But that's who it was. It has to be. I could figure it out. There aren't that many families. I know his name. The police gave it to me. I could just ask my parents and they would remember the family, or not. But I don't want to know. I'm sure already. So what would be the point of asking?"

Finally, she took up the rum from the table. She drank it down in a gulp.

"Fourteen dollars an hour," she said.

"Island rates. I never made that back then."

"It was a racket. It was so much money too. To me, then. God, I was happy with it. I kept a little ledger. Knew what I was doing every night of the week, whose house I was going to, how many hours, who owed me what. It was all right there in the book."

It sounded very satisfying, described that way.

Then, after a time, she said, "This kid, Billy, you're sure you don't know him?"

"I'm sure."

"Never babysat him?"

"Nobody ever asked me to babysit."

She shrugged. "I know it's probably nothing, Jim, but I don't like it."

"Neither do I."

"There's more too. But don't tell me. I don't want to know. I don't like any of it."

I kept thinking she would ask about the fire across the marsh, what it was for.

We had been talking for an hour, maybe, and it was out there burning all the time.

30

The door opened and I saw a suitcase first. Behind it was Maya, who looked like she hadn't slept much. I didn't know what time she went in. I felt I owed an apology or an explanation for my behavior but wasn't sure where to begin or how far back to take it.

"It's time," she said, by way of acknowledging the suitcase. Shannon seemed less convinced and was lingering inside with a coffee. I sensed quickly that all the discussions had already taken place and they had decided what needed to be done.

When there's a baby involved, decisions come easier. Your appetites change, sharpen.

Your appetite for risk, mystery, the unknown, friends, fights, strangers. All of it.

I helped with the bags and asked only once if they were sure. Neither of them seemed too inclined to get into it. There was a kindness in that: in not coming out with it, putting it to words. They trusted me to understand. "Tell Valentina we're sorry," Shannon said. "I'll call her from the road, but if I don't get hold before you see her, just explain we had to get home. Tell her . . . I don't know. She won't be upset, will she, James?"

The last thing to go in the car was Shannon's pregnancy pillow, the long, narrow one that Maya called the snake. It couldn't be folded, apparently. It was laid over the top of their bags. From tail to tongue it must have measured nearly six feet. It was poking into the front seat, resting on the console between them. The kids had come out to wave goodbye, and one of them asked what that thing was. Rami said he would explain it to them but not while I was around. He didn't want to embarrass me, he said. They seemed to think that entirely sensible. They trusted him implicitly, more so all the time.

After the car disappeared past the salt pond, Rami suggested we all go down to the beach to collect seashells. That was what we spent the rest of the afternoon doing.

I couldn't remember another day when we put together such a collection. They were everywhere, in fine condition, and the kids were happy enough to keep at it straight through lunch, so that finally when we remembered to go up to the house, there was no time to put together a real meal. We just slabbed peanut butter on wheat bread and ate standing up, the four of us around the kitchen counter, with the shells spread on a towel Rami laid for that purpose. There must have been three hundred shells altogether.

I checked my phone and saw a missed call from Valentina and a message: "Heard from Shannon. What the hell?" Then, a short time later, another came in: "Coming home tonight. Need anything from the house? Try not to lose anyone else before then, okay?"

An odd idea occurred to me then. We were still standing around the counter, with the shells laid out. The kids were going down the rows polishing them with damp paper towels. I asked Rami if he was the executor of Bruce's estate. Bruce had mentioned it once.

He said that he was. They had done the paperwork a few years ago.

"But it's just for administration of accounts and policies. He has a literary executor. She's named in the documents. Seemed a little ambitious to me at the time, but hell, I don't know, the books must be worth something. The character, maybe. They made a movie after all."

"Have you ever done that sort of thing?"

"Administered an estate? No, have you?"

"Nobody ever asked me."

He thought about it for a moment, agreeing it was odd. "You're a lawyer," he said. "I wonder why he didn't ask you. I've never done it. I hope that I never do. I'd like to die before all of you." He announced it matter-of-factly, as though it were quite ordinary.

I had often thought just the opposite of him. That he would be very old someday. He had one of those faces, the kind that are ready to go on forever, smiling, taking things lightly. And he was usually quite careful about what he ate. He might drink or smoke, and there wasn't much exercise in his routine, but when it came to diet, he was careful.

One of the kids asked what an executor was, and between the two of us we managed to turn out an explanation. Then Rami found a tin of sardines and we all had a few. The kids had never tried sardines, or any tinned fish before, but again, they trusted in him.

———○———

Valentina came home that evening. It was just after dinner, after nightfall, and the kids were already upstairs. She went to visit with them first thing. She stayed up there so long I thought she may have fallen asleep beside them in one of the beds. When they were younger, that used to happen to her, and she would spend the night like that, without meaning to. I would find them in the morning, sleeping in a bunch, like animals, looking very pleased and all of them with the same crease marks across their cheeks because they had slept so heavily the sheets had imprinted right onto their skin.

I was in our bedroom when she came down. I was looking out the window, toward the marsh. There were two fires burning now. They were in the same clearing as before. I didn't mention what I was looking at and she didn't ask and didn't come to see but instead sat on a corner of the bed and looked for a long moment at the wall. Thinking, maybe, how to begin, where she wanted to probe first. There were any number of ways.

"Shannon didn't mention anything about ghosts," she said, finally. "So I assume you kept that part of it to yourself. But she did say there were some strange noises and you've been visiting the jail. With those kids who were arrested. Maybe they had come back around to, I don't know, try scaring you. Maya was scared. So I guess I'm just wondering what the hell is going on, Jim. I'm wondering, and I just can't figure it out."

It sounded like she had figured it out but was keeping her conclusions in reserve.

She fell back onto the bed, her arms spread out at her side. Exasperated, maybe.

Looking at her there, sprawled, a part of me was thinking about crawling onto her.

A strange idea, but that was how I pictured it, getting on the bed, on my knees and palms, and moving slowly across until I was on top of her. Then what? I didn't know.

Instead, I asked if she had been to New York. Asked it casually, like it was nothing, or like it was given that she had been. The question caught her off guard and she turned onto her stomach and looked squarely at me for the first time since entering the room.

"New York? No, why would I have gone there?"

"To see Bruce."

"Did he call? You talked to him?"

I shook my head. No, he hadn't called.

"If there was no word from him," she said, "then why would you ask me that?"

Again, I had the urge to get on the bed but resisted it. I still had my eyes on the two fires that were burning, for one thing. What did they need with two fires? Why not one?

"I've been thinking," I said, "that he was here for you. That was why he came, don't you think? He told me that night he was here for all of us, to see us, but he meant you."

"Which night?"

"The Fourth. The night we fought on the beach. The night he left."

"Why would he be here for me? That's ridiculous."

"He was in love with you. So, to persuade you, maybe."

"Persuade me?"

"To persuade you. Why not?"

"Jesus Christ, a million reasons why not, Jim. Because it's nothing. There was nothing."

"There was once."

Her breathing slowed, as if she were about to fall asleep. She looked away again.

But there was no answer, and I was sure I was right. Had I even suspected it before then? And yet, it wasn't entirely a guess either. Sometimes these things are just known.

They permeate the blood. Then, on the tongue, a taste arrives, metallic and cold.

"It was about five years ago," I said, taking it further.

It was a sudden, muddled certainty, but I had no doubt of it now, not really.

Finally, she said yes, it was about five years ago.

I waited for more and she went on.

"It was when the kids . . . Well, I don't know, it had nothing to do with them, I guess. It had nothing to do with anything. It was one of those awful things. It just . . . happened."

"With Bruce?"

Anger flashed across her eyes. For putting her to it, I figured.

"You've known," she said. "All this time? Why the hell did you never say anything?"

"I didn't know, exactly."

"But you figured there was something?"

"Yes."

The anger was gone suddenly. She sounded like she was really trying to understand.

"It was one night. There was a conference in the city. He was a guest speaker. Some nonsense breakout session. It must have been after his book came out, and after the movie. He was getting famous. I didn't go to hear his talk, and I was feeling bad about that. He came to find me at the bar later on, and, I don't know, I remember I was pretending to have heard his speech, his talk. He knew I was bullshitting. We kept going that way for an hour. It was the first conference I'd gone to since the kids were born. Well, maybe not the first, but the first time I was away, staying at a hotel, alone."

"Only not alone."

"No. Hundreds of people there. And he was one of them."

"The one who took you to bed."

"I took him, if we're being honest. I didn't think anything of it. It felt like . . . nothing."

She was lost in the memory but only for a moment. Then she looked up at me again.

"And you knew, somehow."

I nodded. "I remember when you came home. Thinking there was something."

"But he never told you?"

No, he hadn't. Neither of them had ever spoken about it. They had been very sophisticated. All of us had been. These things happen. In a lifetime, of course they do.

"But I think he was here for you," I said. "This summer, that's why he came."

"To persuade me?"

"To leave with him. To choose him. Maybe just to tell you something. I don't know."

"But he didn't, Jim. He didn't do any of that. He just left."

She was looking at me like a stranger. Like she had that time we had been playing at it, in the room, after Camille had shown up that night, after we'd come home along the beach in the fog and found her there, and afterward Valentina had wanted to play at it.

I remembered then something she had said to me earlier in the summer. That by the time she met my friends, it was too late for them to shape her. She was already formed was the implication. Yet she met me at that same time. What did that mean for me, for my chances?

Maybe that was her appeal, how complete she could seem, how little use she had for me. You would have thought it would change after the kids came, but it never really did. Those foundational things never change, even with kids in the picture.

I told her I was going downstairs. It was cruel, leaving her like that, but I didn't care. I only wanted to sit alone on the porch and have a drink. I said I would come up later and we could talk more, if she wanted, but we didn't need to. If she fell asleep, that was fine, we'd talk in the morning.

But before I could leave, there was one more thing. A conclusion she had drawn.

"I think we should leave," she said. "Tomorrow. Pack up the place, go home."

"All right."

"Rami's going to go to the city for a week, before he flies back."

"You talked to him already?"

"He called me this afternoon."

"Well, I guess it's all planned, then."

"It's not. I'm asking you. But I think we should leave. The summer's over."

"Is he going to come stay with us?"

"Not in New Haven. He's going to New York."

"To stay where? What's he going to do, check into a hotel?"

"I don't know. He'll figure it out. What does it matter where he stays?"

She was right, in a sense. And yet just then it felt very important, and absurd that she hadn't thought to ask him, to find out what his plans were, where he meant to go next.

"I think I'll stay on a few days more," I said.

"Here?"

Yes, that was what I meant. Where else would I go?

She said she would take the kids with her. She thought they were ready to go home.

I agreed, they were, and suggested they could give Rami a ride to the station on the way.

There were three fires burning now. I had been watching them for some time. They never appeared to grow any larger or smaller but just carried on burning evenly, flashing light against the trees now and again and sending up thin columns of smoke.

I had the harpoon on my lap. It hadn't bothered me, finding it there again. I must have left it on the porch knowing I would want to go there once more, to keep watch, and ought to have something in my hands to be busy with, or else I'd sit around drinking all night.

Around midnight the coyote came back, the scrawny one with the ribs showing, and this time he had a friend, another male and almost as skinny. Neither made a move for the carcass. They just sat on the lawn all calm, if not docile, and looked me in the eye for twenty minutes or longer. I was getting ready to throw the harpoon, or to go down and grab them by the scruff if I could get hold and push their snouts down into the bird so they could smell it, know what it was, understand what they were meant to do. But I didn't move, and I didn't go out across the marsh to see who was keeping the fires burning. I didn't do anything. I just sat there with my harpoon and thought about what needed doing around the house. There was plenty to do, and I wasn't the type, like Valentina, to make a list. I just sat and dwelled on the thing for a time and watched the coyotes until finally they bolted, still without the bird, looking hungrier now than ever.

31

She had the kids packed up by ten-thirty. The house cleared out with an efficiency I found startling. It was a cool gray morning and overcast, like a dawn that wouldn't let go. Before getting into the car, she stopped to kiss me but then hesitated, unsure how I would react. She must have thought I was the first man whose wife had ever wanted to feel something new. I couldn't tell her that. I wanted to try but couldn't manage to do it.

After they were gone, I walked once through the house, looking in every room.

Looking for what? Nothing, just to see it, to be overwhelmed by its emptiness.

Closing up the house at the end of the season was always disorienting. Summer seems so tawdry, viewed by the castoffs: towels, blown-out flip-flops, pillowcases that had gone yellow. I ran four loads of laundry, then folded it all away and locked the closets.

Altogether there were four bags of garbage and two of recycling. I drove out to the dump, which was near a ballfield where I played Little League one summer. The seagulls followed you into the drop and circled overhead to see what you were letting go of, then followed you out again as far as the ballfield, where they broke off and returned to pick through the spoils. An efficient operation: I was glad to be a part of it.

After lunch I puttered around for another few hours and found some library books that needed to be returned. I didn't want to have to talk to anyone and just dropped them through the slot beside the front door, then went by the post office and left a note in a PO Box for my cousin George, the one who checked in on the house in the offseason. The note didn't have any special instructions. He had been looking after the place long enough. I just let him know that we were clearing out early and I would tell the hardware store in case he needed to put anything on account there, boarding it up later.

Walking home along the beach, I had an urge to go into the water, a very strong urge.

The only things keeping me from doing it were my shirt and sneakers, which were both old and owed nothing. I took them off and hid them behind a big rock near the bluff and thought if they were still there in the morning and so was I, I'd come back for them.

The water was cooler than it had been all summer. I went out across the harbor. There were boats around and it was a stupid time of day to be swimming, almost dusk, but I got my eyes up every few strokes and saw what was coming. The boats weren't moving fast. They were coasting into the marina, mainly. To swim home, I thought, was a great privilege. I should appreciate it this time, more than I had appreciated it in the past. That's what I was in the middle of trying to do, but inevitably I swam to the point where I thought she must have taken him, where Valentina had led Bruce in her dream.

I felt sure I knew where it was, out past the harbor islands.

I stopped there and tread water so long, it began to feel dangerous, imminent.

Drowning is a euphoric death, we're told. It's the same sensation felt when being strangled, which people will do for pleasure, only nobody shits themselves as they drown, or if they do, there's no sign of it. The water cleans you, washes away the mess.

Finally, I turned for land. It was a distance of a few miles altogether. If you had asked before whether I could swim that far, in open water, I would have said no, not a chance.

Yet I seemed to manage fine. I wasn't even all that tired. I felt I could have gone farther.

----------○----------

I've always taken a long bath at the end of summer. It began when I was young, seven or eight. We were moving around. I entered a new school each year, and the night before a fall semester began, I would take a bath and imagine I was washing away all the joys and liberties I enjoyed up to that moment. A strange indulgence, but nobody ever asked what it was about, so I hadn't felt the need to explain or question it much until it was already hardened into custom, and I couldn't have fathomed going without.

At the beach, we had a claw-foot tub that I liked. It was in the bathroom Shannon and Maya had been using. I noticed something strange, sitting in there. The sketch on the wall—the one Shannon had pointed to that first night after they moved in, of the boy on a potty trainer with the caption, "Les affaires sont les affaires"—was gone.

They must have taken it home with them. A secret they figured nobody would notice or care about.

The idea of it made me laugh. I was glad they had it. Glad they had wanted to take it.

After the water drained, the house was quiet. I couldn't sleep with all that silence and went walking through the rooms again, telling myself I was checking to see what had been missed earlier or left behind. But it seemed like something more, like I was following the absence of a sound, much as you might track a sound itself, to learn the source. In that way, I worked my way through three stories of rooms and downstairs again and was not entirely surprised to look out the window onto the porch and to understand that in fact I wasn't alone at all. There was another person out there. I got closer and saw who it was. It was almost like I was expecting or waiting for her. Ten minutes before I would have said that was preposterous, I wasn't waiting for anything.

"Should I call the police?" I asked. "Tell me what you would do, in my position."

She laughed and looked up at me. Before, as I had come onto the porch, she was looking toward the marsh. She was dressed rather elegantly, in a blue silk shirt, as she had been that first night she showed up at the house, when we were coming back from the pizza parlor and found her there in the living room with Maya. But instead of the white pants she had worn that night, she was wearing shorts now. They were white too.

Camille. She never had mentioned a last name, and I had given up wondering.

"Sit down," she said. "Call them later, if you like. Let's talk first. Do you remember the first time we had a chance to really chat, the two of us? You showed me to the campground. I was sweating hor-rendously all afternoon, and you never mentioned it."

I took one of the rattan chairs and brought it over so that I was be-side her. We were facing the marsh, but you could see the bay, also, to the east. It was the catbird seat.

"Has everybody else gone home?" she asked.

"Yes."

"But not you."

"I'll go to New Haven tomorrow, maybe. Or the next day. I haven't decided."

"And the kids too?"

"They went with their mother."

"So, everybody, then. There's only you."

She was slouched down, looking quite comfortable on the day-bed, which I had earlier stripped of its mattress, so she was sitting di-rectly on the wicker but not seeming to mind it. George would deposit it in the shed, with some of the other furniture, when he got around to it. All the furniture would have to be put away before the winter came.

"Have you been brooding all day?" she asked. It sounded like an innocent question.

"I went for a swim."

"Did I ever tell you about my first husband?" She didn't wait for an answer before continuing. "He used to take long walks. Toward the end, they were longer all the time. When I asked him where he went, he would say, 'Oh, I've been out brooding.' In English, he would say it. He liked that word. He enjoyed it as a pastime. He enjoyed every-thing that was habit. I think that's what came between us, ultimately. I couldn't stand all the routines, but for him they were carved so deep that everything he did became part of them. He was obsessive, really. He would have liked to obsess over me, but I wouldn't allow it. I didn't want to be married in that way. I knew that for certain."

She was waving her hand around as she spoke, almost like she was drawing something in the air: a portrait, maybe, to go alongside the husband she'd decided to tell me about.

"Your first husband," I said.

She held up three fingers, then made a fist. I didn't know what the fist was meant to indicate, maybe that they had all ended. Three husbands, and yet looking at her here, I thought for the first time I was seeing what the others had known: how young she was.

Younger than us all, without a doubt. How could I have seriously questioned it?

"After two marriages," she said, "you can speak with wisdom. But after three, you're forced to admit you know nothing about it. Nothing about why one works and not another. And then you're really free. Although, of course, just the one would be ideal."

"Just the one?"

"The right one. But who's to say, until it's done, which one was right? You live a long time, you grow old, and you think all that will be clear to you someday, but it never is."

"Did you come back here to talk to me about marriage?"

"Would you rather we not talk? There's a long night stretching out before us. Hours and hours. We could fuck, if you think it would make you feel better. Here, or inside, as you wish. I kept expecting you to ask or to find opportunities to rub against me, but you never did. Well, here we are, alone. What shall we do? What would please us best?"

What would please us best . . .

The question reminded me of something. When we were fighting on the beach, I had said to Bruce that it didn't seem he was getting much pleasure out of our company. He had turned on me and asked if that was what I thought it was for—pleasure—and it sounded like nothing could be farther from his mind. And I had felt sorry for him, then.

"I've never cheated on Valentina," I said.

"You sound proud, despite yourself."

"Foolish, maybe. Naive."

She shook her head. "No, you can't help it. You're proud of yourself, even now." After another long pause, she said, "I liked your friends. They were good fun, for a while. In the long term, friendships never last, not when you're together like this, in a house, wrestling with all the things one has to wrestle with, as years go by. The sex gets in the way. Every utopian experiment ever devised collapsed, ultimately, under the pressures of sex. There's no getting around it. That's why you have to stick to family, in the long term. You may not want to discuss it, but you know at least that you have that foundation. The sex is presumed. It's inherent in the exercise, all that shared biology."

"We're not a utopian experiment. We're friends. We were on vacation."

"Yes, well, look how that turned out."

She angled herself back toward the house. Empty, I took her point to be. Everyone gone.

"It's not as though your wife invited him here," she said. "Believe me, I've been with spouses who invite the calamity, and that wasn't yours. She had no wish to hurt you, least of all. Not that I want to sit here and explain a woman's adultery to her husband."

"And yet you came."

"Nothing could be more tedious, that's the truth. Everyone who's ever had a meaningless affair knows how tedious it is. How horribly dull it would be to put into words. And yet that's all the other wants to hear, once it's out. What happened? They want the details, thinking they can re-create it that way. Bring it to life, then snuff it out."

"I didn't ask her for any of that."

"Oh no? Good for you. You were too proud, even, for that, perhaps."

"What about me seems proud to you now?"

She looked me over carefully. There was something probing in her stare, as if she were, with her eyes, lifting my lips to inspect the gums or gripping the flesh in my hindquarters. Some people have a way of looking at you that way. It's not entirely disagreeable, or maybe it ought to be and only the proud and the foolish don't mind it.

"Would you like to know what I think you ought to do with the house?" she asked.

"I think you're going to tell me to burn it."

She smiled, then began to laugh. It was such a high-spirited response, I nearly joined in.

I told her I'd gone to see Billy. He had summoned me, so to speak. I said I spent two mornings in his company and had come away with a distinct impression that he was crazy.

I thought she would want to discuss him, but she pushed straight past the subject.

It was as though she had never heard the name, didn't know him at all. I looked out toward the marsh, where her eyes had moved just then, and was expecting to see another fire burning or maybe three or four, but there was only a deep, quiet darkness.

"Have you ever burned anything?" she asked. "A proper fire, I mean."

"No."

"It's lovely. The fire has a temperament that confounds our efforts to understand, in the ordinary sense. It's like a small child. Do you remember how yours were at that age—three or four—sensing the awful power they might hold over the world but not yet what it ought to mean? With twins, it's unsubtle. A fire is thrilling in the same manner."

She was looking back at the house again, much as she had looked at me. Sizing it up. Speculating how it might react to the flames. Or else I was imagining it, and she was only making conversation. It was polite to make conversation since I had come across her that way, sitting on my porch, and just when I was expecting to have an empty house. I hadn't had the house to myself in years, not since I first inherited the thing and would travel up from the city wondering what to do with it, whether to try to keep it and how, or if I should simply sell. None of the cousins wanted it, and I had never stopped to wonder why. Everything seemed to me such a perfect, stupid coincidence.

"I'm beginning to suspect," I said, "you appeared this summer with an agenda."

She laughed again. This time it was tamer. "Yes, it would seem to you that way."

"Am I wrong?"

"Not wrong, but not so deliberate as that."

"Had you ever met Bruce, really?"

"In a sense. Tell me, what will you do now?"

"With the house?"

"With your wife. Will you drag her to a lot of dreary counseling sessions?"

I hadn't considered it yet. I certainly didn't mean to discuss my plans with her.

But she pushed on. "Did you think about hitting her? One good strike, to try it on?"

"Yes."

"But you didn't."

"What would that have accomplished?"

"Satisfied your hand. What else is there, sometimes?"

She held up the three fingers again, then lowered one, leaving just the two.

"My second husband," she said, "wanted us to see a priest. We hadn't been married by the church, naturally, since I had been married before, and so had he. Neither of us practiced. We hadn't any children to force to Mass on a Sunday. But when the time came it was his only solution: Let's go see the father. He insisted every time we fought."

"We weren't married by the church either."

"But you gave the children a godfather."

"Rami, yes."

"They let you do that, in a church?"

"We were clever about it."

"I imagine you were. Isn't it strange, the things our memories will suggest we do?"

Perhaps to test a theory, or to see what effect it might have, if any, I stood up from where I was sitting, walked into the house, and poured myself a glass of water from the tap. The tap water in Patuxet was exceptionally good. I drank it slowly, with my eyes holding on the waterline, watching the liquid drain to my lips. When it was done, I felt calm and satiated and went back outside to learn whether there would still be anyone there. She was on the same couch, more slouched than before. She looked at me inquisitively and asked if there was any wine. No, I told her, I had drunk the last bottle.

"I'd like to know," I said, "whether you were with Valentina too."

She smiled. "Did we fuck, you mean?"

"Yes."

"You're asking whether the dreams were real."

"I'm not too proud to wonder about my wife. Whatever you think of me."

"But you must have already decided what happened. Tell me, what do you do when you want to know whether you're in a dream? You must have something you look to. Everybody has a little trick, just to bring themselves back to sanity, back to themselves."

"I find something hot. And try to feel it."

"Something hot?"

"A stovetop. A candle."

"I pinch myself," she said. "Right here."

She was pointing to the back of her left thigh, which was very pale.

I leaned over, as though at her suggestion, and ran my hand up her leg. It felt smooth, the skin young. When I reached the point she had indicated, I took her between my fingers and squeezed. She didn't react. She merely observed my hand, dispassionately.

When I had taken my seat again, she asked if I would like to hear a story about something that had happened to her that she thought might be of interest. It was two weeks before, approximately. She had come downstairs one night and noticed that Valentina and I were on the porch. It seemed to her at first that we were fighting, and her instinct was to hold still and merely to watch. Was that rude? She had always enjoyed seeing how people fought. You could learn a good deal that under other circumstances would be denied to you, especially when it came to married couples. Having been married, and more than once, she knew how revealing those moments could be. Whether you kept near to each other or far apart. Who spoke quietly and who shouted. Whether things got physical. Not a beating, but that kind of hatred or desperation which grips the body.

But it turned out, she said, it wasn't a fight at all. We were only dancing.

We had been dancing from the beginning, and she had misinterpreted everything.

It was quite strange listening to her describe the event, which hadn't happened. She said we stayed out there dancing for ten or fifteen minutes. All the while, she was inside, in the dark, watching us. We couldn't possibly have known she was there, yet she felt we were performing for her benefit. That we had been caught, so to speak, and had decided to put on a show. And she felt sure it wasn't the first time it had happened.

"Rather, this was a kind of ritual," she said.

"Like we wait around for people to spy on us?"

"Is that so implausible? Many people—couples—like to perform."

"But it wasn't us. We weren't there."

"It was you. I watched it all."

She sounded so sure, there could be no doubting her account.

"We used to dance," I said. "We were always dancing, at the start."

"Anyone could see that from the way you are together."

"I don't remember when we stopped."

"You never did. I just told you—I saw you there that night."

But what did she mean for me to take from the story? Was I meant

to agree, it had happened? Or did she mean something else by it entirely? She was smiling at me still.

"My third husband," she said, "was always asking to dance when
we fought. He believed that would fix things, if he could only hold on
to me. It didn't matter what I wanted or how I was feeling. He needed
to hold on to me, to remind himself that I was there, maybe, but to me
it felt like being dragged down. Like all his weight was on me."

I knew that feeling. Everybody knows it.

Just as we know what it's like to dance, without having to be told.
Babies understand it.

I told her what I would like, if she was done with her story, was to
know what happened to Bruce. I put it to her quite simply, in those
words, and watched for a reaction. There wasn't much of one. I thought
she may have smiled but wasn't sure.

"Is that what you want to talk about?" she asked.

"You're the one who turned up. I'd like to know what you know
about it."

"How else would this work? Really, Jim. Be reasonable."

She watched me for a time, then reached over, took my hand, and
ran it up her thigh, once more, in exactly the same manner as I had
done it before, on my own initiative. Then she left it at the patch that
I had pinched. There was a faint pulsing there. Maybe the blood had
rushed to that spot and it was still there, waiting for whatever came
next.

Twenty-five. She couldn't possibly have been older. Had I ever been
that young?

I took my hand back and she nodded, as though her point had
been made.

"I think," she said, "you already know what happened to Bruce."

"Do I?"

"Would you like to say? If you're not too proud."

It was a genuine question, not a provocation. That was how I understood it, anyway.

I took my time deciding on the words. "He's dead."

"Yes."

"He died that night."

She smiled, bit her lower lip, then gave way to another laugh while never taking her eye off me. I had never held another person's attention so completely as I held hers.

I was being so careful too. So deliberate. "I killed him."

"How?" she asked. "Do you remember now?"

"With a rock."

"Not a crab shell?"

"A rock. I didn't mean to. We were fighting, and then it was over."

I wasn't talking about dreams any longer. There was no question of that. I was quite awake.

Another smile formed at her mouth, this one more curious, prodding. An invitation.

"It was over?"

"I came down with it. With the rock."

"Just once?"

"Yes. I hit him here."

I pointed to the spot on my own head, picturing his: just above the right ear.

"You didn't mean to," she said, repeating my words. "There was no premeditation."

Hearing her use the term, I was lost for a moment. Premeditation isn't what most people think. According to law, it can arrive in an instant and vanish just as suddenly.

But what was the difference? There weren't any lawyers around. We were just talking.

"And the body?" she asked.

"I don't know."

"Come on, Jim. What's the point of forgetting now? You have time for all that, later."

The moment came back to me: sitting in the mud, watching the surf turn him over. I knew the waves would pull him under. He would be dragged away from the shore. Those currents, wild as they are, were familiar. It felt like something I was watching from a distance. I should have stopped it, should have called for help. He may have been breathing still, or the bleeding may have stopped. Probably he hadn't swallowed too much water at that point. But I didn't do any of that. I simply watched the water grabbing at him, pulling him away. Once he got past the break, either it would sweep him toward the inlet and into the marsh or he would go out into the bay.

"You have it now?" she asked.

She was watching me so curiously, as I remembered it, finally.

"You should have told Valentina," she said. "Imagine having a wife like that, close at hand, and not thinking to ask for help. It was something you could have done together. It could have been like a dance. I saw the two of you dancing, how close you were then. It was lovely, Jim. I wanted that for you. Wanted you to have that moment to return to together, so that when you asked her about all the rest, who fucked whom and when they fucked and who came and who was sorry for it after, all that goddamn foolishness, you would have this other moment to return to. I wanted that. But you didn't ask. You waited to see if the water would clean it all up for you. What a stupid chance to take."

"I should have asked for her help to do what?"

"You know."

"Bury the body?"

"It would have been better, yes."

"Better for whom?"

"Your family, Jim. Your family is the only thing now. Your friends are gone."

I didn't answer. She was entitled to only so much. I was being proud, still.

"You don't know where it is now, do you?"

"He washed into the marsh."

"You're guessing. Hoping. It could be in the marsh. Or floating in the bay. Or washed up on a neighbor's beach. A body, it can be found. What a stupid chance you're taking."

"I know that."

"What if somebody finds it, Jim? That's what I'm asking you now."

"Then they'll find him."

"And you'll what, hire a lawyer? Hope the fiddler crabs take care of it for you before that? It's all the same to me, Jim. There's no way of knowing where the body is now. You could search that marsh for a week, and you still wouldn't know. If I were you, I'd go away. I'd be rid of this: the house, the friends, the stupid games you like to play, the awful green wine you drink. I'd find those ridiculous certificates you gave out, your beach club, and I'd get rid of them too. His bag, his things, they're in the closet still. You know they are. You pretended not to see, but his things are there, on the top shelf of the closet, high, where only he would think to put them. Or you would, maybe. You

were so alike. Practically brothers, but not. If it were me, I would want
to just be finished with the whole thing. The mess of it."

"How?"

"You know how."

"What good would burning it do?"

"The point is to relieve yourself. At a certain point, these things are
a burden."

"They're not."

"You don't owe them anything. They don't owe you either. It's
cleaner that way."

"How is it cleaner?"

"It was an accident. All of it. All of this, a stupid accident."

We were going around in circles. Or perhaps we had come to the
end, without me noticing. I was always missing the end of things, it
seemed to me, and that was the reason I was later filled with sentiment and a conviction that the proportions had been lost, that my
memories and relationships were not so retained as they should be.

"I want to go to sleep," I said. "I'm tired."

She smiled serenely and slouched down farther on the couch. "Oh
Jim, what a mess."

32

When I woke it was still dark, maybe an hour later, but without any moon to judge by.

I got up from the rattan chair and stretched and looked around. Thinking I would see what? The others were gone, as she had said. I went inside, walked through the rooms, feeling their emptiness again, and looked at all the furniture and the decorations we had never chosen. There were so many photographs and portraits around. All these reminders, but after a time you hardly noticed them at all. They might have been anyone's family. Our line had no defining features passed through the ages. No jawlines, no sunken eyes. Just this house and all the paraphernalia, the crazy things mounted on the walls, the harpoons and portraits and maps. The portraits were outdone only by the maps. Maps of the commonwealth, the town, the bay, the coastline, the boating channels. Some were hand-drawn, with markers denoted that hadn't stood for seventy years or more. The channels had all shifted. There were no more lighthouses, not for thirty miles. Now you had to go to Falmouth for the nearest light.

Those maps, what were they good for? Hardly anything these days.

In a desk drawer, I found a small one I commissioned after surveyors had been by five years before and there was some confusion. It charted out the main plot—137 Hazel Drive—from the driveway to the marsh to the beach, and there at the tidemark began a long rhombus carved out from the rest: the NSSC. The Nanumett Sand and Swim Club.

Six shares. Annual dues: seventy-five dollars, habitually waived.

We would never be so close again. Probably we weren't so close now, but it felt like we were for a stretch of days, toward the start, after they all arrived. We made it last as long as it would hold, but there was no point, it was just a game we were playing at. Friendships dissolve. They break apart like any other substance. They deteriorate, sometimes slowly and sometimes all at once, but when you finally see them for what they are, there's a kind of release in that too. I went out to the shed and found the gasoline we stored there in two-gallon canisters, six of them altogether. All summer, I had known they were there but hadn't thought about them until then. Until that night.

I worked my way through the house again, through the rooms, thinking of the priests swinging their incense, chanting the old words that meant nothing but were still a comfort. Then, with the wheelbarrow, I gathered up the brush that Rami and I had collected earlier in the week and carted it up to the house. It wouldn't be right to leave all that for somebody else to take care of later. And I gathered the bird too. The osprey.

The coyotes wouldn't take it, so it would go in with the rest and that would be an end.

Once, when I was young and helping my father clear brush around the yard, one spring weekend when we had come down from Boston, we found a bird like that, dead, and added it to the fire. I remembered how the other birds seemed to know what it was. They were flying overhead, squawking all afternoon, and every now and again one of them would dive down in the direction of the flames, then turn back when the heat reached them. It was strange, and my father hadn't known what to make of it. When I asked him, he told me as much. Maybe it was their way of mourning, he said. A sort of display. He wasn't a rustic person. The brush clearing was a chore he carried out somewhat reluctantly, and my mother used to laugh at him putting on the work gloves.

I kept at it for another hour without a break, working in the dark, going inside and out.

We had some pallets, too, behind the shed. I dragged a half dozen to the porch and leaned them against one another there, in a rough shape that looked something like a pyre. I was sweating a great deal, though it was still dark. The moon came out, and soon after a breeze lifted off the water as though that were the signal, that flash of moonlight.

A breeze was good, I figured. It could only help.

I soaked a rag for a few minutes, then packed it through the mouth of one of the green wine bottles, which seemed the most suitable thing for the job. The glass wasn't very thick, but I didn't know whether thickness would matter in the end. I doubted it would.

I rinsed in the surf before lighting it, then got the rag going and threw it onto the porch. One perfect lob, the most satisfying I ever felt, with a perfect arc, the kind that feels true and right out of the hand and carries on just the way it ought to until the peak.

It came down on the pallets and the glass broke. I think it was the landing that broke the glass, but it may have been the pressure build-ing inside, the heat together with the oil and the gasoline. The pallets went up in a purple whir that was so quick I worried it might extin-guish too soon, but then the flames settled and began to burn more steadily.

I went into the water to watch from there. I didn't know how the flames might carry, or if I may have left a trail of gas and sweat behind me that would draw the fire nearer. Anyway, I wanted to swim. The water was cool, and I didn't go too far in. I just dunked down once, under the surface, and came up again and bobbed and danced around where my toes could still touch the sand below. After a time, there was ash in the air, as there had been the night of the fireworks. I should have gone in with Valentina and the kids. A night swim. Barreling through the surf, splashing wildly, laughing all the while.

I felt relieved, thinking how I would see them soon and by then would be rid of the house. I would pack the Jeep and take it off local roads for the first time in years. When I got to the edge of the salt pond and looked in the mirror, there wouldn't be any gables peeking over the pines. All I would see was open sky, straight through to the bay.

ACKNOWLEDGMENTS

Thanks to:

Jack, Kathy, and Franny Murphy, and that house full of books.

Wareham, Massachusetts, my hometown, my inspiration.

Duvall Osteen and the team at UTA.

Brooke Ehrlich and the team at CAA.

Ibrahim Ahmad, Brian Tart, Kate Stark, Andrea Schulz, Rebecca Marsh, Mary Stone, Emily Fishman, Anna Brill, David Litman, Elizabeth Pham Janowski, Eric Wechter, Francesca Drago, and the rest of the wonderful team at Viking.

My colleagues at *Lit Hub* and *CrimeReads*.

Leonardo, Gisela, Adriana, Ignacio, Paloma, and Rafaela.

Dan, Derek, Tim, Kristen, Emma, Caroline, Liz, and Ian.

Riad, Matt, Mark, Aaron, Phil, and Samer.

Jon, Amy, Arthur, Tilly, Dan, Téa, Nela, Raf, Emily, and Margot.

Shannon, Jeff, and others who occasionally lend names, with apologies.

The Wareham public schools, the Wareham Free Library, the Spinney Memorial Branch, and Marc Anthony's La Pizzeria.

And most of all, Carolina and Eloisa, my beating heart.

100 YEARS of PUBLISHING

Harold K. Guinzburg and George S. Oppenheimer founded Viking in 1925 with the intention of publishing books "with some claim to permanent importance rather than ephemeral popular interest." After merging with B. W. Huebsch, a small publisher with a distinguished catalog, Viking enjoyed almost fifty years of literary and commercial success before merging with Penguin Books in 1975.

Now an imprint of Penguin Random House, Viking specializes in bringing extraordinary works of fiction and nonfiction to a vast readership. In 2025, we celebrate one hundred years of excellence in publishing. Our centennial colophon features the original logo for Viking, created by the renowned American illustrator Rockwell Kent: a Viking ship that evokes enterprise, adventure, and exploration, ideas that inspired the imprint's name at its founding and continue to inspire us.

For more information on Viking's history, authors, and books, please visit penguin.com/viking.